The Chronicles of Álfara:

Book One

The Lights of the North

by

Millie Hardy-Sims

THE Chronicles OF ÁLFARA

the Lights of the North

Table of Contents:

SCANDINAVIAN TERMINOLOGY

Glossary of Scandinavian Terminology

PLACES IN
Heimur

Heimur
"WORLD"
Icelandic. (High-mur).

Dimmtfjall
"DARK MOUNTAIN"
Finnish. (Dim-t-f-yall).

Miðjasvid
"MIDDLE RANGE"
Norwegian. (Mid-yass-vid).

Storflojt
"GREAT FLOOD"
Icelandic. (Store-floy-t).

Kaltopids
"COLD TIPS"
Icelandic. (Kahlt-spid-s).

Einmana
"LONELY"
Icelandic. (Ihn-man-ah).

Norðurtre
"NORTHERN TREES"
Icelandic. (Nurth-uhr-tr).

Vangur
"PADDOCK"

Völlurs
"MEADOWS"

Vesturskove
"WESTERN WOODS"
Icelandic. (Vest-er-skoff).

Austur
"THE EAST"
Norwegian. (Oss-turr).

Hásætishöll
"THRONE HALL"
Norwegian. (Hass-ett-is-hull).

Suðurskog
"SOUTHERN FOREST"
Icelandic. (Suth-ur-skog).

Skógur Hanna Huldu
"SECRET FOREST"
Icelandic. (Skug-ur-hanna-hull-doo).

Stöfnfe
"CITADEL"
Norwegian. (Stoff-in-fe.

6

RACES OF
Heimur

Ljósálfar
"LIGHT ELF"
Icelandic. (L-yoh-sulf-ar).

Banvænn
"MORTAL"
Icelandic. (Ban-veh-nn).

Dökkálfar
"DARK ELF"
Icelandic. (Dock-al-fur).

Nisse
Scandinavian Folklore. (Niss-uh)

Hrafn
"RAVEN"
Icelandic. (H-yaff-n).

Rensdyr
"REINDEER"
Icelandic. (Ren-s-deer).

Björnings
"BEARS"
Icelandic. (B-yuh-urnings).

Leikki
"WILL O' THE WISP"
Finnish. (Lie-key).

Dverger
"DWARVES"
Icelandic. (D-vur-gur).

Ulfurs
"WOLF"
Icelandic. (Uhl-fur).

Huldi
"TROLLS"
Icelandic. (Uhl-dee).

Fe
"FAIRY"
Icelandic. (Fay).

Hjörnings
"UNICORN"
Icelandic. (H-yuh-or-ning).

Myrkur
"SHADOW"
Icelandic. (Mur-kur).

Jätte
"GIANTS"
Swedish. (Yat-uh).

Matardýr
"MEAT BEAST"
Icelandic. (Mat-ar-deer).

NAMES OF
Heimur

Køllungr
"COLD ONE"

Álfara
"ELF"

Einar
"LONE ONE"

Höfðingi
"CHIEF"

Pieni
"SMALL"

Nikkel
"CHOSEN; LIKE A GOD"

Töfrandi
"MAGICAL FRIEND"

Frelsar
"LIBERATOR"

Jörð
"EARTH GODDESS"

Freyja
"ANIMAL GODDESS"

THINGS IN
Heimur

Alder
"AGE"

Gramr
"BLADE"

Kexbers
"BISCUITS"

Sockerbär
"SUGAR BERRY"

Hedalmäk
"FRUIT BREAD"

Dedicated to all the believers

1
Chapter One
IN THE BEGINNING

1 | In the Beginning

*L*ong ago, the world of Heimur was created by the Gods.

These Gods were not terrifying, they did not punish without just cause, nor did they live above their humble beginnings, but they should not be messed with all the same.

They furnished their new world with hundreds of species of animals: some magical, some not. They created Björnings, great furry beasts with their mighty paws and thick jaws, capable of surviving the frozen climates and climbing the densest of trees. They formed the Hvafn, flying beasts of jet black feathers who were easily the most intelligent of all creatures. They made the Rensdyr, great gentle creatures with branches upon their heads, moulded from pure starlight. They invented the Ulfurs, creatures of dense fur and sharp teeth who preferred isolation in the wilderness, but were fiercely protective of those that they trusted. They created Nisse, small, wise, bearded beings, to care for these animals and all of the others, entrusting them with the races they had forged. Then, once the animals had made their home with the Nisse by their sides, the Gods created three great beings in their own image. Of these three great beings in particular, above all of the others, the Gods were most proud.

The first to be created, the Banvænn, they built from the dirt and the earth itself. These beings were much like you and I in appearance and personality. They had life spans of up to 100 years, they lived in houses and had jobs in order to maintain the society which they continuously built for themselves. They did not heed much to the magical elements of the world that surrounded them, and it seems that such ignorance kept them alive for generation after generation. Of course, they could not escape the magical beings with which they shared their homeland, nor the beasts that roamed free around them, but they did not pay them much mind if they did not pay mind to them. They were a simple folk who lived life their way, and had done for centuries.

The second creation of the Gods were forged with the first sun beams of the winter and the crisp frost of a cold morning, manipulated and bent to form petite creatures with pointed ears and large eyes that reflected the lightness of their souls in shades of green, blue and purple. These beings, very different to the Banvænn, were reinforced with the powers of nature and creation. They were given the name Ljósálfar, and were talented in many ways that the Banvænn were not. They made a home within the woods and forests of the world, using their talents to befriend and care for the animals with which they shared their home, using their skills of creation to invent and concoct items to better the world around them. The Gods were proudest of these creations, tending them as one tends a garden and rearing them to reflect the Gods themselves. These were creatures of kindness and fortune as the Gods believed they themselves were. The Ljósálfar took time to care for all around them, although they rarely ventured near the Banvænn and instead kept to themselves inside their enchanted woodlands. The Banvænn began to think of them as nothing but legends, stories to tell their children.

The third and final being that the Gods made in their own image was that of the Dökkálfar, forged from the flame, the ash and the soot. Where Ljósálfar were made from all things light and caring, the Dökkálfar were made from darkness and waste. Their sole purpose was to bring balance to this world that the Gods had lovingly created. In contrast to their light cousins, the Dökkálfar were instead dark in features, their eyes ranging in shades of grey, red and black. They dabbled in nightmarish things such as grief, pain and anguish, stalking shadows where the Ljósálfar dared not tread. They were every part as powerful as the Ljósálfar, but they instead used such powers to cause suffering. Where the Ljósálfar were skilled in creation and loyalty, the Dökkálfar were instead skilled in warfare and manipulation. They favoured isolation over companionship, even with one another, and the darkness of their souls shone through their eyes, causing fear in all who looked upon them. The Gods had been most unhappy to unleash such beings upon the world, but it had to be done in order to balance this new world. For, without darkness there cannot be light.

Heimur, the world where all of these races dwelled, was made up of four great forests, three mountain ranges, two citadels and a whole lot of nothing in between. The three great beings of the world, the Ljósálfar, the Dokkalfar and the Banvænn, rarely ventured outside of their own territories. The forests were dominated by the light-giving Ljósálfar, the mountains by the secretive and calculating Dökkálfar, and the citadels by the Banvænn. The only creatures to venture outside of what they knew would be the animals and the lesser beings, such as Nisse, the Huldi and the Dverger. They alone did not fear the beings who dominated Heimur in their tribes, and instead sought to simply survive and share their talents in moderation.

The four great forests: Norðurtre, Suðurskog, Vesturskove and Skógur Hanna Huldu, made up the four points of the compass. Norðurtre, the Northern trees, were barren and habitable only by a select few Ljósálfar who could survive there. It was mostly inhabited by Björnings and was surrounded by the Kaltspids, the larger of the three mountain ranges. To the West was Vesturskove, the forest of the hardier Ljósálfar who made their living tending to the Ulfur who roamed there. They were deemed as the most feral to all of those who spoke of the Vesturskoven, wild beings with sharp teeth and wide eyes, hunters who ran in packs.

To the South, past the small Banvænn Citadel of
Einmana, was the water forest of Suðurskog, where the
resident Ljósálfar made their living from the great river
Storflojt that flowed through their centre. Here they
fished in the evergiving waves and built boats to sail
along, keeping the peace. Sudurskog was bordered by the
mountain range of Dimmtfjall, the smallest of the ranges,
where the Dökkálfar were negligible in their appearance
and presence and shared their home with the small,
bearded, quick-to-anger Dverger. These Dökkálfar were
the most insignificant of their brethren, and as a result
passed beyond most common memory. In the very centre
of Heimur was the largest mountain range, the Miðjasvid,
which the majority of Dökkálfar called home. It spanned
most of Heimur's land mass, meaning the Dökkálfar
could live their isolated preferential life in

companionable solitude, equal halves together and apart, just how they liked it.

Finally, to the East, spanned the largest Banvænn Citadel, that of Stöfnfé. Stöfnfé was home to most of the Banvænn population, and bore high stone walls to keep the Ljósálfar and the Dökkálfar out. These walls had been built as the Great Forest of Secrets in the East, Skógur Hanna Huldu, held all manner of things inside, things the Banvænn did not care to acknowledge. Skógur Hanna Huldu was home to the most powerful of Ljósálfar, and within the dark trees there came many whispers throughout the years, whispers the Banvænn wished not to heed.

For centuries the three great beings lived in parallel harmony, continuing their own lives and existences far away from one another. The Banvænn built villages for their growing population and busied themselves creating civilisation without the use of magic. The Ljósálfar hid within the woodlands and forests, tending to the animals in their charge and using their powers of creation to care for the nature around them. The Dökkálfar, unhappy with their lot, retreated into the caves and mountains to live in the darkness that reflected their very souls, plotting and damning. All was manageably content in the world that the Gods had created.

Until, that is, the rise of Kollungr.

Kollungr, a particularly powerful Dökkálfar, resented the Ljósálfar for all that they had been given by the Gods. For years he watched them, jealous of their temperament and the love they held. He saw their contentment in their homes, their use of magic to tend to the Earth and its occupants, and Kollungr was envious. He wanted what they had, and he was going to take it.

Kollungr stood menacingly above all, the tallest and most intimidating of the Dökkálfar. The appearance of the Dökkálfar race had been lost in living memory, but legend states that Kollungr had the palest skin, the darkest eyes and the sharpest of smiles. His armour was said to be forged from a dying star, his gramr from the cold moonlight of a blue moon. It was no wonder, really, that the Dökkálfar had rallied to follow him.

Whereas before the Dökkálfar had lived in isolation, they now found themselves uniting under the desire of Kollungr, either by force or by decision. They envisioned the images he painted with his promises, craved the joy that he swore must come from living in the forests and towns occupied by the Ljósálfar and Banvænn, and so they followed Kollungr into battle. To begin with the war was small. Kollungr and his Dökkálfar followers made a point of attacking small pockets of Banvænn, not wanting to prompt a rebellion but instead hoping to take what was not theirs with stealth. They were, after all, skilled in logic and warfare. They could plan in secret and execute their plans without so much as a whisper. However, word of the coup eventually reached the Ljósálfar, carried on the wind by elemental spirits who wished to help stop an onslaught. The Ljósálfar assembled in order to stop the coming war, to prevent the abolition of their homeland and all they knew and held dear. The Gods had given them compassion and they were set to use it.

The Ljósálfar rallied together to make a stand against Kollungr and his army of darkness. They appointed a King where none had been before, electing the strongest and most trusted amongst them to act on their behalf:

Einar. Einar was a humble Ljósálfar from the Northern forests. Though he had never seen battle, as there had never been a need, Einar was logical and fearless. He had the best interests of his people at heart, and so his people believed in him in return. It was his fierce loyalty to the survival of not only his own people, but the Banvænn too, and all of the creatures who shared their great earth, that had won him the crown and the title that would destroy the wicked, envious Kollungr.

The Banvænn did not thank Einar for his bravery and sacrifice, nor did they wish to aid the onslaught. Instead, the limited minded, short sighted Banvænn retreated from the slaughter, wanting to keep their people away from the magic and the uncertainty. They sealed all borders against magical beings and raised their children with no knowledge of magic. For generations to come they would have no knowledge nor pay a mind to the battles between light and dark. All the Banvænn would know would be all that was before them. There would be no need to acknowledge the whispers in the darkness or the light carriers who brought news.

For one hundred years, generation after generation, the Banvænn remained separate from the waging war. They did not live as long as their magical brethren, and so through the generations they eventually, simply, forgot why they carried such a deep seated fear of anything different from them to begin with. This was how they liked it, and so it would be. The wars of spiritual beings meant nothing to them, nor did the simple lives of the Banvænn.

And so it was, after a century of battle, that Einar and Kollungr met in the final field of war. It was not just a war for the Earth any longer, but a war for light in the darkness. The conflict of light and dark is as common as night and day, but this final stand was far more dangerous and all-consuming. The future of Heimur hung in the balance. The battle was long and bloody, a century of slaughter and bloodshed, with Dökkálfar and Ljósálfar losing their lives on both sides. Einar grew desperate to defeat Kollungr and stop him and his followers plunging the delicate world into darkness. Countless of each kind had lived and died for the cause. Einar wanted nothing more than to end it for the sake of themselves. He decided to put an end to it once and for all, choosing to finally meet Kollungr on the field himself, to lay waste to this dictatorship once and for all. One night, on a snowy plain, the two ancient, exhausted, Alven Kings alone fought to the last man, and it was during their duel that Einar and Kollungr defeated one another, and ended the uprising with their martyrdom.

As their spilled blood mixed, the black of Kollungr and the white of Einar, their many followers laid down their arms and agreed on peace for the first time in a century. Kollungr had been foolish, even the Dökkálfar could, at last, see that, and many had simply followed him out of fear. The Dökkálfar returned to their caves and mountains and balance was once more restored. The Banvænn must have known that the battle was over, they must have felt a shift in the world around them, but they were content to continue to ignore the existence of magic. They had made a life for themselves in the past century, ignorant of the plights of others, and so it would stay for the good of their survival.

After the battle, the Ljósálfar retreated back into their forests, and this time they too closed their borders. The Dökkálfar, what was left of them, faded from mind and memory. For centuries to come neither Ljósálfar nor

Banvænn spoke of the war. If there were Dökkálfar still out there, they would not know, nor did they care. The defeat had been enough to deter the Dökkálfar from ever uprising again.

At least, so they thought.

THE WINDS OF ADVENTURE

2 | The Winds of Adventure

*O*ver the centuries that followed the battle of Kollungr and Einar, of light and dark, memories faded and what had once been true, soon became nothing but legend.

The Ljósálfar, who each could live for centuries at a time, grew generation after generation in their passive existence. With each new generation the memory of the great battle faded just a little more until, at last, it was simply a great story. Ljósálfar parents still spoke of the story to their children, but that was all it was: a story with which to go to sleep in the evening, or to warn Ljósálfar children of straying too far from what was deemed acceptable and normal. Adventure was for stories, not for deeds, and that was how it should be. Very rarely did Ljósálfar children ignore such a warning, and so they lived in harmonious oblivion, not one of them wishing to seek out the Banvænn who so readily ignored their existence, nor the mythical Dökkálfar who had caused so much trouble and heartache. The darkness was defeated, so why should new generations wish for its return?

And so our story truly begins, with a Ljósálfar child who had been raised on the Legend of Kollungr and Einar, told the story as just that, and raised to not ask further questions. Or so her parents wished.

Álfara, however, was not the type of Ljósálfar child to let stories simply be stories.

The leaves on the tips of the branches waved in the winds as the breeze brushed through Skógur Hanna Huldu, teasing with the promise of adventure that rarely ever came. This particular corner of the forest was dense with great trees that had been growing thick and fast for thousands of years. Ever reaching towards the sky, they seemed to long for an escape that they could never bear witness to. Instead, they remained content to be the backdrop and the home to the beings who lived amongst their roots: the small creatures who foraged there, the occasional Hvafn that made a nest in their welcoming arms, the Ljósálfar who went about their business in the ancient presence of the trees around them.

On this particularly windy morning, a petite Ljósálfar, slight even for her race, bounded confidently from one branch to another. She seemed to trust the trees to always catch her as she moved nimbly between them, and the least they could do was oblige. After all, what else were they doing? The Ljósálfar frequently danced across their bows this way. She was much at home in the treetops, making her way, as she often did, to a particularly gnarly ancient fir on the outskirts of Skógur Hanna Huldu. Her path was well trodden, her course well known, and she swiftly moved in the pursuit of her endeavour. Eventually, with the wind on her side, she made it to her favourite fir and nestled herself contentedly in the topmost branch, leaning back against the mossy chair she had fashioned over the days and years she had frequented her perch. She hung one leg over the edge of the branch freely as she often did, pulling her pack from her shoulder and depositing it in a crevice in the tree trunk.

She was slight, as all Ljósálfar were known to be, and stood only about 5 feet at full height. She was petite, too, her dainty features prominent in the light of the rising sun. It was early morning, her favourite time, and her bronzed skin glittered with what seemed to be gold dust. That was the mark of a true Ljósálfar. They had, after all, been made from sunbeams. She had long, thick, curled auburn hair that complimented her golden complexion, and her nose turned up at the end in a perky snub, a splash of freckles across it. Her pointed ears stuck out from her curls, a defining feature of her race, and her golden eyes shone brightly as she peered through the trees. It was a recognisable trait of the Ljósálfar to have shining eyes, but Álfara's were particularly bright. Her mother always told her it was because she was curious, that her eyes sparkled mischievously in search of her next adventure, adventures she shouldn't be seeking. Her father would always shake his head at this and warn her mother not to put ideas in her head.

Álfara loved her family dearly, but she did not always agree with them. Her mother and father were both in the business of building, her father Arkin being head of a company that specialised in building furniture, and her mother Oline a weaver who made drapery for the houses Arkin furnished. Álfara's older brother Aksel was set to join Arkin in the trade as soon as he came of age, 200, which he would do in the next decade. Álfara, at 150, was much more content to spend her time climbing trees and exploring her small corner of the world she longed to see more of. She knew when she, too, reached 200 she would join the trade as well, and already knew how to build something from nothing, but that wasn't what Álfara truly wanted to do. She wanted to leave Skógur Hanna Huldu, to see the world. Her grandmother often shook her head at Álfara's spirit, wondering where she had got it from.

"It's certainly not from my side of the family," Alvissa would say as she shook her ringleted head at her granddaughter, then turning to her son-in-law with a shameful look in her eyes, "Must be from Arkin's stock."

Álfara didn't tell her family where she went everyday. She wouldn't know where to start if she was going to tell them. After what had happened to Aksel all those years ago, when Álfara had been only just 80, her family did not trust the Banvænn and forbade Álfara to go anywhere near the walls of Stöfnfé.

It had been a particularly grey day, and Aksel and Álfara had been roaming the woods playing hide-and-seek amongst the roots in a rare moment of Aksel being kind to his younger sister. The trees loved it when they played these games, whispering amongst themselves about how much fun they looked. Álfara had been hiding in one of her favourite trees as Aksel searched for her. It was a particularly tall tree and Álfara found that she was skinny enough to fit inside a gap in the bark, meaning it was harder for Aksel to find her. Aksel began calling her name, drawing attention to where he was, and as Álfara was giggling to herself that she was sure to win, it had suddenly become quiet below. Eerily so. The trees had stopped whispering and the birds had stopped singing. Concerned, Álfara had peered out of her hiding place and down to where she had last seen Aksel. To her horror, she had seen a group of boys with rounded ears surrounding him. They were punching him, kicking him, and one even spit at her brother, who was laid on the ground trying to cover his face and protect his own pointed ears. Álfara fought to free herself from her hiding place as the assault continued, but by the time she managed to wriggle out and shimmy down the tree, the boys had left. One had fallen over a tree root that had been placed specifically, and they had fled back in the direction of Stöfnfé.

Álfara ran to her brother where he lay beaten and bloodied on the ground. He was barely conscious, and Álfara screamed for someone to come and help. Thankfully, her screams had been heard by some Ljósálfar who had been foraging nearby, and Aksel had been treated for his wounds by the healers.

Since that day, however, Arkin and Oline banned Aksel and Álfara from ever venturing near Stöfnfé again. They had gotten too close, they said, and the worst could have happened.

"The Banvænn are simple folk. They fear what they do not understand," Arkin had explained, "Our people have a great history with the Banvænn, and they are suspicious of us. Stay away from Stöfnfé, do not put yourselves in danger like that again."

To Álfara, it had seemed that in this age of peace from the Dökkálfar, the Ljósálfar simply needed somebody else to fear and to worry themselves with. Kollungr and his uprising had made them wary of anything and anyone who was different.

Aksel had heeded their father's warning without hesitation, and Álfara had tried, but as the decades passed she had found herself drawn to Stöfnfé with an unspeakable urgency. Banvænn did not live as long as Ljósálfar, and so Álfara was sure those boys who had so brutally attacked Aksel were old and gone now, and so it was that in the last decade that Álfara had tested the waters. Day by day, year by year, she had ventured a little closer to Stöfnfé via the treetops where she felt most safe.

It had taken a long time to get to where she was now, nestled in the branches at the top of her favourite nest tree on the very outskirts of Skógur Hanna Huldu, but she had finally made it. What was more, her family had no idea where she went, and that was how Álfara wanted to keep it. For all they knew she was off learning a trade. If only they knew.

The truth was, Álfara was fascinated by the Banvænn who dwelled within Stöfnfé. From where she was she could see over their tall walls and enjoyed long days of simply observing them going about their daily business. They were funny, she thought, in the ways they did things. Much like the Ljósálfar they were builders and weavers and storytellers. They had families and ate similar foods and even looked similar, although their ears were comically flat at the tops and their skin didn't sparkle like the dawn sunlight. They had plain, pale skin, and hair in various ordinary earthy shades, but something about them drew Álfara to them.

She was yet to find out why, but, as the winds blew around her as she perched atop her tree, watching a farming family on the very edge of the Stöfnfé citadel as the grandfather and grandson fed their livestock, Álfara couldn't help but feel that the breeze brought the promise of a long awaited change, a promise of adventure.

The winds continued to blow through the treetops as Álfara sat upon her perch. Hour after hour she watched the Banvænn from her makeshift treetop watchtower, content to live through those she could see far below. The same Stöfnfé grandfather had now gone inside his little hut, his grandson also gone from view, and Álfara was left to watch the animals roam their small holding. She knew not how long she had been there, nor the time of day, save for the early signs of sunset beginning to shine on the horizon. She knew she should head home soon before her family wondered where she was. *Just a little longer...* she kept telling herself. They wouldn't miss her until it got really dark, and she could always run home to make up the time that lapsed as she stayed in her nest. After all, there was nothing in Skógur Hanna Huldu who would seriously seek to harm her. The Ljósálfar were in charge of these woods, and the animals all knew it. She was as safe as could be in her comforting forest shroud. Since the defeat of the Dökkálfar centuries ago, even the very darkness that fell after sundown was not frightening, but instead comforting, like a great embrace surrounding her. She had no worries heading home in the dark.

As evening truly began to fall, Álfara began her descent from the tree. She was not brave, nor stupid, enough to try and make her way home through the branches that had been her path on the way to her perch now that it was dark. She would only safely achieve her pursuit through the daylight.

Álfara was every bit as nimble descending the trunk, nonetheless, and soon reached the ground. She stroked the tree bark to thank it for its safe clutch, and it groaned a little in response, stretching its long branches in the wind that had persisted throughout the day. She gathered her bag around her hip and adjusted the strap on her shoulder, tucking her curls back under her flopped, pointed hat and turning in what she knew to be the direction of home.

She had barely made a few steps, however, when there was the sound of a twig snapping behind her. Álfara, fearing a forgetful creature in the unknown rising darkness, turned towards the noise and scanned the forest trunks with her bright eyes. Instinctively, she dropped to a crouching position, ready to run or pounce, whatever it took. She knew how to fight. She had grown up with a brother, and her father knew his way around the use of his gramr, a long curved blade that he kept in the chimney flue. Álfara just needed to know what she was up against in the impending gloom. She didn't know what she expected to see: an animal, another Ljósálfar, just the wind, but whatever it was, she had not expected to see a Banvænn boy standing before her in the dusk shroud.

3
Chapter Three
THE CALL OF THE UNKNOWN

3 | The Call of the Unknown

Álfara froze in the position she had assumed,

staring at him. She hardly dared to move as the boy

turned his copper eyes towards her. He was just about the

same height as her, and seemed as surprised to see her as

she was him. He had a round, pale face and dark hair that

stuck out from under his red stocking hat, which sat at an

angle on his head. Like Álfara, the boy also had a

smattering of freckles across his nose, though his was

more pear-shaped and didn't stick out as far as hers. He

cocked his head on one side in a quizzical manner as he

43

looked at her, stuck as she was in the uncomfortable stooped position in which she had landed. He didn't seem scary or threatening, nothing like those big boys who had once beaten up Aksel and caused Álfara's family to fear the Banvænn with everything they had. No, he was much softer, much more approachable. In fact, he seemed just as nervous to be standing opposite her as she was of standing opposite him.

For a long, silent moment neither of them moved. They stared at each other, eyes wide and fearful.

Then, with no fear and a slight accent to his voice, one different to that of the Ljósálfar, the boy asked, "Who are you?"

Álfara swallowed, straightening her back at long last and trying to decide exactly what to say or do. On the one hand, she could try to run away from the boy. She was faster and probably lighter on her feet, being an elf, and she knew the woods far better than him, but he was built larger, his legs longer. What if he followed her? What if she accidentally led him to her family and the rest of her people? On the other hand, and the hand she seemed most inclined towards, Álfara could stand her ground and attempt to intimidate the boy until he left. Álfara was petite, but she had a way with words that could be unparalleled amongst her own kind.

On a third hand, had she one, she could simply answer his question. He may, after all, not be as bad as her family had told her or she had seen. She had been watching the Banvænn for most of her life, especially in the last few years, and they didn't seem to be all as bad as she remembered. This boy particularly... His family lived on the farm on the outskirts. She watched him feed the chickens as though he were as normal as she and her

Ljósálfar people. She recognised him now after looking at him for a while.

"Who are you?" The boy asked again, clearly unphased by the amount of time it was taking Álfara to answer, or run, or react in any way. He took a bold step closer to her and she recoiled a little.

"Álfara." She said in a small voice. Her words had come from her mouth before she could stop them, as though guided by fate. She scowled at her own tongues betrayal.

"What's wrong with your ears?" The boy raised a querying eyebrow as he looked beneath her askew cap.

Álfara indignantly straightened it and folded her arms over her velvet green coat. "Nothing. What's wrong with yours?" She said with heavy sass in her voice.

The boy put his mittened hands to his ears to feel them. "Mine aren't pointed?" He said, as though it were obvious.

Álfara realised what he had meant. Of course he had different ears to her. The Banvænn had not been blessed with the points that identified the Ljósálfar and Dökkálfar from them. The Banvænn had plain, rounded ears that often stuck out a bit far. She, too, put protective hands over her ears. Before she could respond to him, either with the truth or something else, he continued speaking.

"Are you an elf?!" He took an excited step towards her, and she matched his step in moving away. She would crash into her tree trunk soon if she continued retreating, she knew that much in her stunned state of being.

"What's an elf?" She asked. It was her turn to cock her head in question. She had never heard such a term in her long, long life. Her curiosity got the better of her as she was intrigued after the answer.

"You know... magical folk who live in these woods?" The boy was speaking as though it were obvious. "Pointed ears, special powers."

Álfara scoffed in amusement. "Powers?" She said, giggling. "You make us sound like Gods." She rolled her emerald eyes in spite of herself.

"So you are an elf!" The boy's face lit up and he took another step. Álfara did not step back this time. She was as intrigued by the boy as he seemed to be by her.

"I'm not an elf." She scowled, offended. She had only just heard this term but already it was offending her, like slang. It seemed so short, so unmagical, hardly worthy of her people's long and ancient history. "I'm a Ljósálfar." She stuck out her bottom jaw defiantly, eager to educate him.

The boy nodded excitedly. "That's it! I've wanted to meet a Ljósálfar since I was young enough to hear the old stories."

"Old stories?" Álfara was growing more and more intrigued by the moment. She knew in the back of her mind that she should still try to get away... but he wasn't exactly a threat. From what she could see, anyway, he was a normal boy. A normal boy with red cheeks and sticky-out rounded ears.

"About the Ljósálfar and the battle with the Dökkálfar." The boy was beaming. He spoke very fast, very enthusiastically. "I've read all the stories. They don't teach us them, of course, but I found an old book in the library. Your history sounds so cool, but..." He hesitated, and Álfara found herself hooked on every word he was saying about her own people. "But we never believed you were real. Not anymore. We all thought you'd died out, that's why I wasn't afraid to walk in the woods." He fidgeted now from foot to foot, picking at a loose woollen strand on his mitten.

Álfara blinked at him, trying to work him out. "Well, the Ljósálfar definitely have not died out in Skógur Hanna Huldu." Her words came out in a protective tone. She folded her arms tighter around her torso and stood her ground.

"Wow!" The boy beamed even wider, if that was at all possible, his fidgeting ceased as excitement took hold. "I'm Nikkel." He said, thrusting out his mittened hand so quickly that Álfara jumped backwards in alarm. Her back slammed into the tree trunk and she rubbed the back of her neck.

"Sorry!" Nikkel said, his mittened hands now over his mouth. "I didn't mean to scare you!"

"You didn't scare me." Álfara said in a sulky tone, pushing herself away from the tree trunk and clenching her fists, her stance as wide and strong as she could make it, indignant. However, once she had determined that he was not about to burn her, Álfara too reached out a tentative hand. He was nothing like his kin, at least not the ones who Álfara had met before. She unclenched her fists and softened her stance. He was not a threat to her, nor she to him. She swallowed and, her mind made up, took his hand in hers. Their fingers touched, and their hands shook together, a perfect fit.

"Hej Nikkel." Álfara found herself smiling all of a sudden. Something about Nikkel, despite his race and the differences between them, made her feel at ease. He had a welcoming, soothing aura. "I'm Álfara." She said. All around them, their hands still held together, the wind picked up with a feeling of urgency, of change. Nikkel seemed to feel it too, turning his round nose up to where the leaves were being blown past them. As soon as he released Álfara's fingers, the wind softened. It seemed to be an omen of something unspoken. Álfara looked down at her fingers for a moment. She had never felt a connection like that. Nor, it seemed, had Nikkel. He looked at his own fingertips and then at Álfara in confusion. He had clearly never felt a connection like that either, let alone a magical one. It was an odd occurrence, one that left them both speechless. At the very least, however, it brought Álfara back to her senses. She crossed her arms again and picked up her pack, hastening to return home before much longer.

"I shouldn't be talking to you." She said hurriedly, glancing around quickly as though her parents were about to jump from the treetops. The darkness was gathering thick and fast around them now. She knew she would be in trouble if she didn't hurry home soon. As fascinated as she was by Nikkel, she knew better than to outstay her welcome in the presence of Banvænn. She looked back at him, her head no longer on a swivel. "It's getting dark..." She paused, frowning. "What are you even doing here? Especially now you know Ljósálfar still exist." Part of her couldn't believe the Banvænn were so ignorant as to think her race had died out. She kept that thought to herself, however.

"My grandfather told me to go for a walk and get out from under his feet." Nikkel kicked the forest ground a little guiltily, his mittened hands sliding into his pockets and his shoulders shrugging. "He didn't specify to stay within Stöfnfé walls, though." He peered up at Álfara from beneath his hat, his red cheeks all the more flushed and a mischievous glint in his eyes.

"I think he assumed that was implied." Álfara giggled in spite of herself. Nikkel looked at her, eyes shining, and shrugged.

"He should have said."

Álfara grinned. She was finding a kindred spirit in this Banvænn boy, whether it was allowed or not. The more she stayed, the less she wanted to leave. Even as the dim light of dusk grew stronger around them, the winds of change were on Álfara's mind. They had blown strong when they had touched. This encounter with the Banvænn boy was more than just chance, and the longer she stayed the more she saw that.

"You live on the farm just inside the wall?" She didn't know why she was making small-talk now. She didn't know why she was not heading home.

"Yes..." It was Nikkel's turn to frown as he realised she recognised him, "How did you...?"

"I like to watch you." Álfara said casually, pointing to the treetops. Nikkel looked up to where her nest could vaguely be seen in the highest branch.

"Whoa." Nikkel said in a tone that was part awestruck, part something else.

Álfara realised her words could be construed as a little creepy and changed tact, "Not in a weird way." She added quickly. "I find Banvænn fascinating."

"Why?" It was Nikkel's turn to scoff. "We're nothing special. No powers, no pointy ears..." He gestured at her ears again and she covered them reflexively. Nikkel dropped his gesture as she did, realising it was perhaps a point of contention between them. Or at least, he was making it awkward for her. "Just... us."

Álfara smiled at him. It was a genuine smile, wide and warm. He couldn't help but smile back.

"I think 'just you' could change a lot of things." She said truthfully. The winds of change were on her mind again, but, as she stood looking at Nikkel, the thought of her family at home crept in. "I really should go." She tried to lace her tone with explanation, wanting Nikkel to know it wasn't because of him. "My family..." She looked over her shoulder again as though her family were about to jump out at them, then looked apologetically back at Nikkel. "They don't know I come this far out, away from home."

Nikkel smiled his wide smile again. "So I'm not alone in deceiving my family?"

Álfara blushed. Not as bright as he, but bright enough. She nodded, then shook her head, conflicted.

"It's different with my family." She admitted, unsure why she was speaking so freely. Nikkel frowned at her by means of asking for more information. Álfara rubbed her arm absent-mindedly, thinking. "My older brother... he was attacked by some Banvænn boys." She had told him before she knew what she was really saying. Nikkel's eyes widened in sympathy.

"That's awful." He said. "On behalf of my people, I'm sorry." He pulled his hat from his head and rang it in his hands before him, clearly affected by her words. He was so genuine that Álfara could not badmouth his race further.

Álfara blinked at him, watching his hands and noticing just how nervous he became. It was clear from that one reaction that her family was entirely wrong about Banvænn. They had generalised them as a race, despised the whole people without reason. Just like Ljósálfar, they were individual. The thought gave her comfort.

"It was a long time ago." Álfara shrugged, feeling herself a little choked up by his humble reaction. "Before you were born, probably. Given how our life spans are different."

"Of course." Nikkel said, putting his hat back around his ears. He had messy grey blonde hair beneath it that greatly contrasted his copper eyes. He cleared his throat. "I wish you didn't have to go." He admitted. He was blushing again, his cheeks rosy, which made Álfara smile at him in an endearing fashion.

"I'll be back tomorrow." She admitted, once again feeling her words came out from her mouth before her mind had triggered them. Without knowing it, she was setting up a rendezvous. She found herself excited for it. Nikkel grinned.

"I'll see you then, Álfara." His eyes sparkled as he met hers. Álfara smiled back.

"I'll see you." She replied. Then, before she could change her mind and linger longer, more than she should, she turned her back on Nikkel and made her way through the forest in the direction of her home. She dared glance back after she had walked a few steps to check if Nikkel was following. He wasn't. She could see him framed against the edge of the forest, the lights from Stöfnfé behind him, silhouetting him. Álfara, once again guided by something beyond her control, raised a hand in farewell. It was an automatic gesture that felt just the perfect level of correct. Without hesitation, Nikkel matched her gesture, proving her point.

The winds of change were growing around them again, blowing leaves about their feet and catching on Álfara's long curls. She looked up and into the breeze, reading the signs as clear as day. She would see the Banvænn boy again, standing as he was right where she had left him. Their meeting was meant to be. They were linked by something unspoken.

The call of the unknown.

4

Chapter Four
DANGERS UNTOLD

4 | Dangers Untold

$\mathcal{I}$t didn't take long for Nikkel and Álfara to become fast friends.

The day after their meeting, Álfara had all but run back to her tree on the outskirts of Skógur Hanna Huldu. She couldn't wait to see Nikkel, to learn more about him, about the Banvænn, about why the winds of change were so invested in their meeting. Nikkel must have felt the same because he was already there and waiting by the time Álfara had made it through the forest. He wasn't in her nest, of course, as by his own admission he could not 'climb a tree to save his life'. That was the first thing Álfara needed to teach him, and teach him she did, though he only got as high as the lower branches. Still, it was more of a secret if they were not out on the floor for anyone or anything to see. Nikkel seemed to enjoy being up the tree once he had made it. He had never had a head for heights, apparently, but now he never wanted to get down.

"In the unlikely event that anyone should ever be searching for me," Nikkel said proudly, clutching his branch tightly with his hands and his knees, his cheeks flushed, "I shall be up in the skies and out of reach."

That first day they had spent hours upon hours trading differences about their lives. Álfara had learned that Nikkel's parents had died when he was a boy from some sort of fever. He had been raised by his grandfather,

Osmon, for as long as he could remember. Osmon was a kind and just man, but he liked things to be done a certain way. Nikkel had received his share of beatings upon occasion for letting harm come to the livestock on the farm by accident. He said he sometimes struggled to remember everything. Álfara suggested he should keep a list, to which he just laughed.

"One time, I left the henhouse door unlocked and all but one were carried away by a ræv." Nikkel admitted, picking as he spoke at a loose bit of bark. He was clearly affected by the folly of his youth.

"Have you left the henhouse open since?" Álfara asked him from where she sat in the branch above his. He shook his head. "Then you learned a lesson. Life is all about lessons." She passed him a bunch of berries that she had produced from her pack. They were bright pink in colour and tasted like fruit punch. Nikkel had never tasted anything as sweet. His diet was limited to meat and potatoes grown on the Stöfnfé farms.

"What are they?" He asked eagerly as the sweet sugar dripped down his chin.

Álfara laughed at him and handed him a handkerchief. "Sockerbär." She explained between giggles.

"We have plain old blueberries in Stöfnfé, and they rarely ever flower. Not often enough to satisfy my craving for sweet substances, anyway." He complained, wiping his chin and then eating three more sockerbär in quick succession, his eyes squeezing shut with glee. Álfara chuckled at him, and their conversation had turned to talk of what exactly the Banvænn ate in Stöfnfé. To Álfara, their diet sounded boring and bland.

"Bread, usually made of rough grains. Cereal of the same grains. Milk if we get it ourselves. Eggs from the chickens that the ræv have not run off with..." Nikkel covered the clear regret in his voice with yet another sockerbär. "We eat the chickens too when they grow too old to produce eggs."

Álfara frowned at this. It was not the custom of Ljósálfar to eat the animals with which they shared their world. She did not like to imagine it, so when Nikkel began to talk about the matardýr who the Banvænn raised purely for slaughter, Álfara had to ask him to stop, her mittened hands covering her ears.

"Do you not eat meat?" Nikkel had asked in surprise.

"No." Álfara sounded offended, and Nikkel feared for the first time that this might be the end of their budding friendship. Álfara, however, was not as shallow as to stop talking to him purely on that basis. "We take the gifts that the animals give us, so we do eat eggs and milk and we use furs if they are shed…" She thumbed the fur rim to her hat. "Otherwise, we have no right to kill those with whom we coexist. That has always been our way. We are guardians, not executioners." She tailed off as she realised Nikkel was surveying her with a strange expression, like he was seeing her for the first time. This was of course not the case, so she frowned at him. "What?" She said protectively.

"My people were so wrong about Ljósálfar." He shook his head as she spoke, his voice heavy with the past prejudice of his people.

"How so?" Álfara asked. She knew she should be cautious in her questioning, but she was too curious to care.

"In all the old stories, for instance, they talk of elves...
sorry," Nikkel noticed how Álfara flinched at the word,
"Ljósálfar..." He corrected. They had talked about the
derogatory terms that the Banvænn applied to the
Ljósálfar in their stories. 'Elf' was a word to describe a
being of mischief and madness, which the Ljósálfar were
most certainly not. Álfara had explained this to him and
he had apologised, vowing to try and change what he
could.

"I just have to get used to the strange term." Álfara
explained. "Continue."

"Well, all the old stories have us believe that Ljósálfar
are dangerous, not to be trusted, that they'll use their
powers for destruction and they endanger Banvænn."
Nikkel shook his head in disgust. "But if you don't even
kill animals, how am I expected to believe you would ever

cause harm to my people by accident, let alone on
purpose!"

Álfara considered his words. It was true that her
people had a history of violence, but it was never violence
against the Banvænn. It provoked violence against the
Dökkálfar, with good reason and in self defence. They
would have killed not just the Ljósálfar but the Banvænn
too. Álfara shivered as she thought about it. She was
conflicted between educating Nikkel whilst maintaining
her own dignity and protecting the integrity of the race of
his friend.

"What do your stories say of the Dökkálfar?" Álfara
asked in a hushed tone. The trees fell silent for a moment
at the name of the darkness. She knew she should not
speak of it. Álfara looked up at the treetops
apologetically, which was enough for them to resume

their whispering. She met Nikkel's eyes and held his gaze, intrigued once more. Nikkel seemed to pick up on the nervous energy surrounding the Dökkálfar, and tried to be as tactful as possible in his response. He drew his knees up to his chin and rested it upon them for a moment as he thought about what to say. The trees continued their anxious whispering, putting Álfara on edge.

"The stories say that they once tried to consume the world in darkness. That they're the reason the Banvænn retreated behind our high walls, both in Stöfnfé and across the world in Einmana." Nikkel frowned as he tried to remember, speaking his words mostly to his chubby knees.

"Do they say how they were defeated?" Álfara picked at a loose strand on her green velutinous coat, avoiding his eyes and ignoring the ever-growing agitated hisses of the leaves around them.

Nikkel shook his head, causing Álfara to look at him.

"They don't." He admitted. "Our stories end there."

The trees fell silent again as though in satisfaction.

"Of course..." Álfara nodded, understanding. "The Banvænn retreated into their cities and blocked out the rest of the world. They wanted nothing to do with the war, or the stories that came from it." She remembered from the legends spoken amongst her own people that the Banvænn had built their walls to have nothing to do with the battles raging around them. Nikkel nodded.

"How did it end? The war?" Nikkel asked, his eyes wide with eagerness. Álfara surveyed his expression. He really didn't know. That much was obvious. Perhaps her telling him would be beneficial to the future of her people, and maybe even peace between them and the Banvænn.

Álfara shifted from her branch down to the one below upon which Nikkel was sitting. She moved effortlessly, like a bird, and curled up her legs before him in a mirror of his pose, though she did so in a far more dainty manner than Nikkel would ever have managed.

"It was King Einar the Fearless." She said, her eyes shining. She knew the story better than anything. It was told to all Ljósálfar from birth, woven into them like thread on a tapestry. Nikkel's own eyes widened with anticipation. "The Ljósálfar don't have royalty, not usually, but we appointed him as our leader as he was the strongest of body and of mind." She hopped onto her feet on the branch, effortlessly balancing as she acted out her story, jabbing and sashaying. Nikkel managed to marvel at her swift footedness for all of a millisecond before becoming once more consumed by the story. "The Dverger who dwell in the forests built him armour of precious ore with which he could battle Kollungr. The Jätte came down from their mountains to forge him a gramr of beams from the New Moon, filled with new beginnings and promises. The last of the Hjörnings, a great silver beast with a horn of diamond, became his steed. He was named Frelser, the saviour, and save us he did." Nikkel watched in amazement as Álfara continued to hop around the branch like a robin, acting out the battle. "Einar rode Frelsar into the field to meet Kollungr. All around him the Ljósálfar rallied to his side. The battle went on for a hundred days, for Ljósálfar and Dökkálfar do not tire easily, until finally the last Hjörning fell and Einar was forced to meet Kollungr on foot. Both sides had lost so many. Einar wanted this to be over. He and Kollungr fought in hand-to-hand combat, gramr against gramr, until at long last they struck each other down." Álfara sank back into a sitting position, her story all but ended. Nikkel was staring at her with a wide mouth and even wider eyes. "The Dökkálfar, what remained, retreated into their caves and probably died out. The Ljósálfar returned to the life that we knew... and clearly, the Banvænn remained oblivious." She gently shut Nikkel's mouth for him. He shook his head to clear it.

"I hate that they don't tell us the full story!" Nikkel broke out of his awed stupor and lay back on his branch in frustration. "Fifteen years I have lived, and fifteen years I have gone without that story!" His hands were on his head, still processing it. Álfara giggled and climbed back onto her higher branch, eating sockerbär whilst she waited for Nikkel to regain his composure. It took him a while, so excited was he by the epic tale of their history. Eventually, he sat up and looked at her. "How cool it must be to live the life you have lived, Álfara! To be a part of this race of such goodness! Such a virtue!"

Álfara blushed a little. She had never really thought about it before. One-hundred and fifty years she had been on this earth, and not once had she thought about how that had occurred. "I suppose so." She admitted with a humble shrug. This was another reason to like Nikkel, to risk trouble in order for their friendship to grow. He showed her new perspectives that she had never before seen.

Over the following days and weeks within which Nikkel and Álfara learned about one another, sitting as they did in what was now their tree and trading stories about their own lives, they both grew closer in a way that neither had ever experienced or imagined. The winds had been right, it seemed. Something about destiny had meant them to meet that day, and as the days continued the stronger their destiny grew.

So it was, as their bond grew, that Álfara wished to tell Nikkel everything about herself. He knew all of the superficial things, the fights she had with her brother, her desires for the future, the strictness of her grandmother... but now she wanted him to know more about her. The real her. The her she hid from everyone. Nikkel, it seemed, felt the same, for when Álfara broached the subject he agreed in a heartbeat.

"What is a secret you've never told anyone?" Álfara asked on one particularly drizzly day. They were both huddled on a wider branch, still not very high but high enough, beneath an umbrella of a canopy that shielded them both from the rain. As they talked they had been experimenting with their combined foods, adding Ljósálfar nuts and berries to Banvænn breads. The concoctions that they had created resembled something that was not only edible but delicious, too, a sort of sweetened cake with many flavours.

"A secret?" Nikkel asked through his mouthful of the recipe they had jointly entitled *hedalmäk*. He swallowed and frowned at her as best he could from where she sat right beside him.

"Mmhmm." Álfara replied.

"Well, why don't you go first, whilst I think?" Nikkel asked with a cheeky edge to the smile he gave her. Álfara narrowed her eyes back at him, an act that scrunched her nose, but then she thought about it. She knew what her secret was. It had plagued her since she was a girl, and though her family had suspicions, she had never told them the truth.

Álfara took a deep breath. Even though she had only known Nikkel for a few weeks, he already felt more important to her than anyone outside of her family. They had an unspoken bond that she had never experienced, one sponsored, it seemed, by the winds of change that continuously blew around them. "Alright." She started, turning on the thick branch to face him. The rain itself seemed to hush around them a little as she spoke, as though it too wished to hear. Álfara picked at the loose strand on her coat once again, a habit she had adopted when she was nervous. "Since I was a girl," She began, "I have had dreams…" She looked down and away from Nikkel's face, not wanting to read anything in his expression. She did not know herself if her dreams meant anything at all. "Dreams beyond ordinary night musings.

Dreams about... about..." She stuttered as she looked for words heavy enough to explain what she meant, "Darkness, and despair, and things a Ljósálfar should not be dreaming about. The world was swallowed in darkness, and all I knew was terror." She blinked. "But I have had other dreams filled with light, many lights, of all colours of the rainbow. They fill the sky in waves of every hue and I feel calmed when I see them... but then... then the darkness consumes them and I cannot get them back." She dared look up at Nikkel. "Which probably sounds crazy."

Her voice tailed off as she realised Nikkel was staring at her. She didn't know what she had expected from his reaction. Some laughter, or something light-hearted. She had not expected him to be staring at her with wider eyes than she had ever seen, his last piece of his precious hedalmäk subconsciously crushed in his fist.

"What?" She asked tentatively. Her grandmother had always taught her not to use 'what' as a question, but it felt the right word in this moment, at the sight of his expression, when all other words failed her.

"Álfara..." He dropped the hedalmäk so that it fell from the tree to the soggy ground below. "I have had those dreams." He spoke in a hushed tone.

It was Álfara's turn to widen her eyes.

"What?!" She repeated, this time in shock and surprise. "You have?"

"Yes. The lights in the sky, the darkness consuming them. I have dreamt, too, of a ruined hall. I stand in the middle of it and ahead of me are three creatures: a Björning, a Hvafn and..."

"An Ulfur!" Álfara finished his sentence for him. She too had seen the hall. She too had seen the great stone creatures. She covered her mouth in shock, her eyes as wide as his now.

"There was a feeling too... a feeling of..." He gabbled, and he and Álfara together finished the sentence.

"Dangers untold." They spoke in unison before staring at one another incredulously.

"What does this mean?!" Nikkel demanded, as though Álfara would know. She shook her head weakly.

"I do not know." She said. She had never told a soul about her dreams, though she had dreamed the same dream countless times throughout her long, long life so far. It was more than just a dream to her. It was as if she existed on another plane of existence. She felt what it felt like to marvel at the rainbowed waves, how horrible it was to watch the lights be consumed by darkness. She knew the fear and confusion that came from the ruined hall and the three stone creatures. Nikkel seemed to be thinking the same thing as she was at the moment. Neither of them had ever seen a real-life hall like the one in the dream, nor lights in the sky, nor real darkness. Yet they knew what it felt like.

"This must mean something!" Álfara said before she could stop herself. "For a Ljósálfar and a Banvænn to be dreaming the same dream, then finding each other by chance... it must mean something!" She spoke fast, filled with eagerness and a touch of fear.

The fear grew inside her when a voice replied to her from down on the ground, below their wide tree branch.

"It means that you are in a world of trouble."

It was Aksel. Her brother.

5
Chapter Five
THE DESCENDANT
OF EINAR

5 | The Descendant of Einar

*A*ksel wasted no time in betraying Álfara to their parents.

After he had made himself known, spying on them as he had been, he had taken off running through the woods. Álfara had made her apologies to Nikkel, told him to get out of Skógur Hanna Huldu and return to Stöfnfé where he would be safe, and she had leaped from the tree and taken off running after her brother. But Aksel had always been faster, swifter, stronger. He reached home long before Álfara had. By the time she had burst into the kitchen of their little cottage in the heart of Skógur Hanna Huldu, Aksel was half-way through his treacherous account. She could tell by the expressions on her mother, father and grandmother's faces. Álfara stood her ground as she tried to catch her breath, her eyes fixed on the ground. She knew there was nothing she could say or do to convince them that Aksel was lying. Aksel was the golden child, he never lied.

Nevertheless, her mother thought it necessary to ask.

"Is this true, Álfara?" Oline asked her daughter in a tone that told Álfara she already knew the answer. She was still holding a crock pot and had been in the process of scrubbing it.

"Is what true Mama?" Álfara asked. She didn't attempt to meet her mother's eye. Out of the corner of her field of vision she could see that her father was sitting on a kitchen chair, his stockinged feet up on the guard before the fire. His boots had obviously leaked whilst he was working today. To the other side of Álfara, sitting near where Aksel was standing triumphantly, was their grandmother. She had been in the process of knitting, but now her needles were clutched in her hands like daggers. Álfara avoided looking at all of them, studying the flagstone floor as she was.

"What Aksel is saying." Oline continued, her nostrils flaring.

"What is Aksel saying?" Álfara asked, a touch of cheek in her tone that she did not intend to utter. She ducked to avoid the scrubbing brush that came flying at her head. It hit the door behind her with a sudsy 'bang!'.

"Don't play coy with us, Álfara!" Oline shouted. "You were on the outskirts of the forest with a... with a..." She suddenly gasped and sank into the chair that Arkin only just vacated in time. Oline clutched her bosom, the crock pot still held in her other hand. Álfara wondered momentarily if she could dodge that as easily as the brush in case that was to be her mother's next weapon of choice.

"With a Banvænn." Alvissa finished Oline's sentence in a cold voice. Alvissa was not the usual grandmother type. She was not warm and feeling, with pockets filled with sockerbär or good things for her grandchildren. She was cold and distant, her head stuck in the past. The only member of the family Alvissa doted upon was Aksel, who greatly resembled her long dead husband Ásgeir. She told him often and Álfara had grown up knowing that, in her grandmother's eyes, she would be forever inferior to her brother. From all she knew, Álfara did not resemble any of her long dead ancestors. She was unique in her colouring and temperament, something her father often spoke of fondly. Oline and Alvissa were not as fond. Oline certainly favoured her mother. She, too, lived in the past, though she had not lived as long as Alvissa and so had much less past within which to dwell.

"She's not even listening to us." Oline scoffed. Álfara forced herself to break out of her thoughts of her family and look at them instead.

"Yes it is true." She said, her fists clenching at the sight of the smug look on her brother's face. "But it's not how you think. He's not like his people. His people aren't even like the stories. Not anymore."

"Hark at her!" Alvissa cried, throwing her arms up in exaggeration. She still held her knitting needles and

Aksel stepped to the side to avoid being accidentally skewered. "She thinks she knows the Banvænn because of one Banvænn boy!"

"You know our history with the Banvænn, child." Álfara's father said wearily. He had given up his chair for his wife and so now leaned against the guard instead. "You know what they did to your brother. What they did to your grandfather."

"Allegedly." Álfara said before she could stop herself. She looked up worriedly after the word left her lips. They all looked as shocked as she had expected. "I mean... of course what happened to Aksel was real. But what happened to grandfather... I just... I'm not sure."

"Not sure!" Alvissa waved her arms again and Álfara took a step back this time. "Were you there, child?!"

"No, grandmother." Álfara hung her head a little, but her eyes were still trained on the old woman. "But I doubt the Banvænn would have set upon grandfather like you say. The ones who attacked Aksel were a rarity amongst the Banvænn. They are not a cruel race. They do not despise us as you have always said." Álfara was desperate to get them to understand, though she knew it was fruitless.

"Listen to her. One boy and she's singing their praises." Oline shook her head, greatly resembling her own mother as she too threw up her arms. Álfara flinched at the sight of the crock pot being lifted, but Oline did not launch it at her. Yet.

"You know nothing about the Banvænn, Álfara." Alvissa shouted. She was dominating this interaction now. "You are so like your father, always wanting to see the good in people." Alvissa shot her son-in-law a look. Arkin, too, hung his head.

"Why is that a bad thing?!" Álfara suddenly felt anger beyond anything she had ever experienced. She clenched her fists so tight that her nails dug into her palms. "I'd much rather see the good in people than the bad! What a miserable existence that must be to only see the bad side!" She had shouted much louder than she had intended. Her family stared back at her, shocked. Álfara was such a gentle soul. She never raised her voice, never. In her 150 years of life she had probably only grown angry once or twice.

"Go to your room." Oline said. She didn't shout, yet her voice was so much worse. It was dripping with danger. "Stay there until you have remembered that you are a Ljósálfar and not a Banvænn. That your loyalties are to this family, this race, this homeland. Not them. You will never see this boy again, do you hear me?"

Álfara had never been sent away before. It was a great disgrace amongst the Ljósálfar to be sent away from anything. Álfara looked to her dad for support, but as always the gentle-minded Arkin looked to the ground. He was not going to argue with Oline and Alvissa when they were a combined force.

"Fine." Álfara glared at her family. "At least I have the guts to speak my mind and not just follow the river like sheep!" Álfara left the room before Oline could add any more punishment. She heard their conversation continue as she climbed the rough wooden stairs of their cottage and then the ladder to the attic room that she called her own.

Their cottage was not overly large and grand, but it was cosy enough for a family of five. It was carved into the trunk of an enormous oak and had been in the family since the Ljósálfar had first come to Skógur Hanna Huldu. There were three grand rooms on the ground floor, the largest of which had been furnished into quarters for Alvissa as the matriarch of the family. The other two were the kitchen and the family room, the latter also functioning as some form of family archive or library. On the first floor were two more bedrooms belonging to Aksel and to Oline and Arkin. A small bathroom of sorts was squeezed between them, right behind the permanently fixed ladder that led up to Álfara's attic. The rungs of the ladder looked as though they would soon fall apart from overuse, but it had been standing for hundreds of years that way and would surely remain that way for hundreds more, however long the family wanted to stay there. It was a cosy home, a quiet home, a peaceful home. At least when the family let it be so.

Álfara loved her room the most. It was the smallest room by far due to the fact the trunk narrowed as it grew taller, but Álfara loved it all the same. She had an old armchair in one corner next to her stack of old books, each containing a different legend or myth of Heimur. Her favourite was a tome about the Gods. She had read that one so many times that the spine had been in need of repair for fifty years. Beside her little bed was her little wardrobe, though she wore the same variation of outfit every day: her green velour coat, her red hide trousers (given to her with the blessing of the matardýr they had come from), her fur-lined green hat (the fur of which was gifted from a ræv after she had rescued it's pup from a river), and her Ljósálfar boots. They were made of brown plant-based material, well-worn, and had a telltale Ljósálfar turn-up on the toes. It was a great tradition amongst the Ljósálfar to gift their offspring with such boots. It would happen on the eve of their fiftieth birthday, and age that marked a great rite of passage amongst their people. They were always imbued with some form of magic, for they grew with the Ljósálfar throughout their lives.

Álfara's favourite part of her room was the small window that led out onto the branch. This had been where she had first learned to climb. As a child she had fit easily through the small hole, but now she was grown it was more of a squeeze. Nonetheless, she was often visited by small birds who could fit through the window, and she welcomed their companionship. There were no birds out there today, however. It could be due to the rain but most likely it was due to the shouting they had heard

94

from inside the house. Birds did not like conflict and so endeavoured to stay as far away from it as possible.

Álfara emerged from her trapdoor and threw herself down on her bed immediately, letting the wood slam shut behind her. She had never felt more disgraced in her whole life. She stared up at her ceiling, entwined as it was with branches and leaves, and glowered. This was all Aksel's fault. Not just that he had spied on her, which angered her all on its own, but that he had then told on her and turned her own family against her. She hated him, and it was very rare for Ljósálfar to hate anyone or anything within their own community. Ljósálfar were, by nature, companionable. They made it their life's dedication to be there for and with their own kind. Yet, as she glared at the ceiling, Álfara felt sure the feeling she felt for her brother was hatred.

They had never got along. As children, Aksel would often lead Álfara out into the woods on his walks, knowing she wanted to be with him, and then leave her there to find her way home. He would never get the blame for it, though. Of course not. It was always 'silly Álfara' who got lost on the path. Álfara wondered if she should thank her brother for that. Because of his neglect and his mistreatment of her, she had learned all manner of secret passages through the forest. Clearly, Aksel had grown jealous of her knowledge. How else would he have found her nest tree? Why else would he seek to follow her? He had wanted to get her into trouble, she was sure of it. As a child she may have forgiven him, but for being almost a man, at 199, Aksel sure could be cruel and childish.

Álfara punched the air in front of her, imagining her fist sinking into her brother's smug and handsome face.

She couldn't wait for him to find a wife and move out. Or would he? He was the oldest, he had the rights to this house once their parents were gone. Would he and his smug-faced future wife and smug-faced children come to live here? Álfara shuddered at the thought. All the more reason to leave. Her family may be content to stay here in Skógur Hanna Huldu. Safe. She wanted more.

In all of the drama of the last few hours, Álfara had paid no mind to what had happened up in the tree with Nikkel. Just before Aksel had ruined everything, Nikkel had confessed that he and Álfara had been having the same dreams. Surely that meant something? But what? Álfara wished she could ask somebody about it, perhaps her father, but she dared not speak of it now. Álfara suddenly felt hot tears sting her cheeks. She rolled over on top of her blankets as she watched the wind pick up outside the window, knocking a branch against the glass as though wanting to come in. Álfara found herself wondering, as tears dripped onto her pillow, if the winds of change were actually the winds of change, or if she had simply wanted them to be. Surely, after all that had happened today, nothing was ever going to change.

Álfara must have dozed off because she woke up hours later to a soft sound at her trapdoor. She squinted into what was now the dim darkness of dusk at the area where she entered and exited her room. The trapdoor looked quite still, but through the darkness she could make out a large book placed just to the side of the hatch. Álfara sat up, wiping the dried tears from her cheeks, and crept across her floor to the book. As she picked it up, the candle on her bedside sprung into life. As a Ljósálfar, Álfara possessed the ability to always have light in the darkness. She was grateful for that ability as the flame danced, happy to be alive. Álfara brushed a layer of dust off of the cover of the book and read the title, written as it was in Aldarin: *SECRETS OF EINAR.*

Álfara frowned further. She had read every book in their family library and had never once come across this. Her father must have sneaked it up to her room from somewhere where he kept it hidden. Nobody else in her family would do her such a kindness, so it could only be him. Álfara sat cross-legged on her bed, her boots still on and the heavy book balanced between her knees, and opened the aged front cover. As she did, a dusty note fell out. She recognised the markings on the paper as her father's handwriting, confirming her theory, and the ink was fairly fresh. Clearly this was something her father wanted to tell her without risking the wrath of Alvissa or Oline.

All that was written on the scrap of paper were four numbers: 1823.

For a moment Álfara stared at them, wondering what on earth they meant. Was it a year? If it was, it was far, far in the future. A code? Why would her father be writing in code? Then her eyes focused on the page the paper had slipped out of. It was the table of contents, and there, on page 1823, were three words: *DESCENDANTS OF EINAR.*

Wondering if she would ever stop frowning, Álfara put down the scrap of paper and turned the thick, heavy book all the way to page 1823. Sure enough, there was the title in bold at the top: *DESCENDANTS OF EINAR.*

Álfara settled in to read.

Although he did not take a wife, it is said that the Great King Einar the Fearless had at least four children. Three, his sons, were killed alongside him in the Battle for Heimur against the darkness and the forces of Kollungr. The fourth, a daughter, fled into Austur and was believed to have perished within.

Austur was the great forest that spread out from the small holding of Skógur Hanna Huldu. Hardly anyone lived there, as through the years it had grown wild and dangerous. It was said that some Ljósálfar had thrived there, though over the years the forest had driven them mad. Many who dwelled in Skógur Hanna Huldu fancied their chances with the Banvænn more than those in Austur.

Although it has never been confirmed, there are some Ljósálfar who have come to believe that King Einar's daughter was pregnant at the time of her flight, and that spread

throughout Heimur there are descendants of Einar who possess

his greatness. It has never been confirmed, but there have been

accounts of individual Ljósálfar who possess the powers Einar

himself had. Strength in battle. Patience. Virtue. And, above

all, foresight. These descendants of Einar have been known to

have prophetic dreams about the darkness returning and the

Dökkálfar rising, though such an occurrence is yet to come to

pass.

Beneath the passage in a swirly handwriting that Álfara did not recognise were three words. Three words that, as she read them, made Álfara gasp: *Know your truth.*

6
Chapter Six
DARKNESS RISING

6 | Darkness Rising

Álfara hardly dared to believe it. Could this be true? Were her dreams of the coloured lights prophetic, and furthermore did they mark her out as a descendent of Einar himself?! Was her father finally trying to tell her something she should always have known? Was her connection with Nikkel something important? Was he, too, a descendant? Álfara found her head was spinning with endless questions. The heavy book slid off her lap and onto the floor as she got to her feet, desperate to pace, to walk, to do something to calm the hundreds of thoughts that were banging against her skull.

Descendants had strength.

That was Aksel.

Descendants were patient and virtuous.

That was her father.

Descendants possess foresight.

That was her. Álfara.

She was a descendant of Einar, as was Nikkel. Even as a Banvænn... something must have happened somewhere to contaminate his genetics.

Álfara thought hard. He had not known his parents. What if one of them had been a Ljósálfar? Álfara sank down on her bed for a moment, clutching her head as though trying to keep her thoughts still and in one place. Why had her father chosen now to tell her all of this? Did he know about Nikkel all along? Álfara wanted to ask him, to get to the bottom of it. She got to her feet with a great sense of determination. So what if she had been banished to her room? This was important!

She was halfway to the trapdoor when she stopped. It would not end well, surely, if she stormed in now. Her mother and grandmother would not hear her out. There was a reason her father had given her the book in secret. Álfara turned back away from the trapdoor and dropped to her knees in front of where the old book had fallen. She turned it over carefully. To her horror, or surprise, the page about Einar's descendants slid out, severed at the spine. Was this a sign? Álfara decided to go with that logic more than it had been her fault that it had fallen apart. She took the page and read it again, then opened her wardrobe and pulled out her satchel. She carefully slipped the page inside, ready to show Nikkel if ever she saw him again. She *would* see him again. She just had to work out *how*.

Álfara was standing in the middle of her room trying to work out what to do for the best, dealing with this great wave of change in her mind, when she first heard it.

Whoosh.

She looked at the window. The sound seemed to be that of a large bird swooping down onto the branch outside. Only, this sound was far louder. Álfara cautiously crossed to the window, her satchel still in her hand, and peered out into the dim dusky grey of the sky outside. There was no bird to be seen. Nothing at all to be seen, really.

Whoosh. Whoosh.

There it was again, twice this time. Álfara cupped her eyes against the glass and really peered outside. Ljósálfar had exceptionally good eyesight by race but even with that she saw nothing.

But she heard it.

Another *whoosh*, and then a sudden BANG on the roof above her head that made her step back from the window. It sounded like an enormous creature landing just feet from her head. Then there came the scrabbling. A horrible scratchy sound that Álfara knew to be claws. Knew without seeing. Whether it was instinct or something else she did not know, but Álfara did know one thing. She had to get out of here.

Álfara had only just managed to lift the heavy wooden trapdoor and place her booted foot on the top rung when, to her horror, the window opposite was smashed into a thousand pieces. Álfara ducked and managed to avoid the worst of the glass, just getting a cut on her cheek, but it was the least of her worries. Coming through the broken window, heart stoppingly, was a creature Álfara had never seen before. She had, however, read about it. *A living shadow.*

It was pitch black, legible even against the greying sky outside, and took a form similar to Álfara. It was tall with two arms and two legs, standing on its two feet with its one head held high. It held a shadow blade in its hand and slunk down from the windowsill and into the room. Álfara did not know how well it could see. She wasn't going to stick around to find out. Álfara slid down the ladder, missing rungs as she did, and down the stairs to the ground floor, just as above her she heard the creature making a horrible guttural howling noise.

"Álfara!"

Arkin's voice came from the direction of the kitchen. He came running through to her. One look at him told Álfara that he had already been battling these shadows. He had blood leaking from his nose and mouth and he was out of breath.

"Father!" Álfara cried as Arkin hooked her under the arm and half-dragged her in the direction of the door. "I read the book...I know about...!"

"Shh!" Arkin hissed. "Don't let them hear." His eyes were filled with panic and warning. Álfara nodded, keeping her mouth shut.

"What are they?" She asked as Arkin led her out of the door.

"The darkness is returning." Arkin said with a shake of his head. He was still standing in the doorway as he pushed Álfara out into the crisp cold of dusk. All around there were cries and screams and further *whoosh* sounds. That shadow in Álfara's room had not been the only one, it seemed. Álfara looked around her in terror. Everywhere she looked there were Ljósálfar running, screaming, fighting. Then, she felt a cold silver object being pushed into her hand from her father. She looked to him and saw, with astonishment, that he had pushed the shining hilt of his own gramr into her hand.

"Run." Arkin told Álfara. "Run!"

"But...?" She made to say as she looked at the gramr.

"You need it more than I." Arkin said, his voice thick with emotion. Álfara's eyes widened as she realised what that meant.

"Papa...!"

"Go, Álfara!" Arkin was already stepping back into the house, his mind made up.

"Mama, Aksel...!" Álfara asked, dithering between running and staying to help her father fight. Something about Arkin's expression told Álfara what she did not want to hear. A single tear dripped down Arkin's bloodstained cheek.

"Run." He said again. He gave her one of his warm smiles, the ones that Álfara had always expected from her father, before slamming the door behind himself and disappearing back into their home.

Álfara took a step forward, wanting to enter the home and help, but a sudden *whoosh* and a ball of fire stopped her. It flew from the sky and crashed at her feet, setting the front door of her beloved cottage on fire, and the light from the explosion showed many more shadow beings running through the woods towards her. Álfara flung herself backwards, away from the fire, and scrambled to regain her footing before the beings were upon her. Inside her house she could hear her father battling the creature. Torn, Álfara dithered for another moment. Every fibre of her being wanted to run inside, to help her father, but she knew it was hopeless. What help was she against shadow beings?

Álfara succeeded in getting to her feet and turned in the opposite direction, running as fast as she could through the forest. Tears obscured her vision as she tripped and stumbled over tree roots, crashing into

112

trunks in her despair and fear. She knew not how far she ran, nor for how long. All around her, her people screamed and cried out for help, fighting with what they could to defend against the shadows. Some had gramr's, like Arkin, that they had kept hidden. Álfara wished she had told Arkin to take it back. At least then he may stand a small chance.

Was this all coincidence that she had learned the truth of her ancestry and then the darkness had descended? What had the book said, after all.

These descendants of Einar have been known to have prophetic dreams about the darkness returning and the Dökkálfar rising, though such an occurrence is yet to come to pass.

Was this the occurrence coming to pass at long last? Was this the darkness of which she had dreamed?

Álfara stopped running. The screams and pleas had been left far, far, behind, and Álfara needed to find her bearings. This was a new part of the forest to her, or at least in the darkness it felt like it. For the first time Álfara realised that this darkness really was dark. Rather than greys and blues and purples, the sky was black. There were no stars. The only light was from the fires burning far in the distance as the shadow beings destroyed what had remained of her home. Álfara felt her emotions overcome her. As sobs racked her body, she sank against a tree trunk and slid down it, crumpling in a heap upon the roots. She held her knees against her chest and wept for her family, her father, her mother. Even her grandmother and brother. All gone. Was she an orphan now? Would she ever know family again?

For almost an hour Álfara sobbed against the tree, the same questions swirling around and around her mind, until at long last she made a decision.

If she no longer had family, she was going to make one. Nikkel needed to know what she had found out. He needed to know what had happened.

With a pit in her stomach, Álfara hoped he did not know first hand. Would these shadows attack Stöfnfé too? Were the Banvænn a threat as the Ljósálfar were?

Álfara decided she had no time to waste. She slung her satchel over her back and tucked the gramr into her belt, hoping she would never have to use it, and began to scale the tree against which she had sought support. At least from the treetops she may be able to get her bearings. She would be able to see the light of Stöfnfé in the distance. She wondered, too, if those things could climb like she could. She did not wish to find out.

From her treetop perch Álfara could see more of the destruction that was occurring in her home. It was far away, at least, but she could still hear the screams from where she was. Álfara pulled her hat down over her ears in an attempt to block out the sounds. She couldn't strive forwards if she was always looking back. Scanning the horizon, she managed to make out the faint yellow glow of Stöfnfé. Nikkel's farm was right on the outskirts. She wouldn't have to go too far into the citadel to find him, for which she was grateful. If the Banvænn were as prejudiced as the Ljósálfar, she would be strung up in a museum before she could speak.

Ensuring that her father's gramr - with a wrench in her heart she realised this may be the last piece of him -

was strapped tightly into her belt, Álfara began to leap from her treetop to the next. This was something she was good at. This was something that she could focus upon. The wind blew around her as she made her way, stinging her eyes as it froze the tears that threatened to fall from them. Álfara tried not to think of all she had lost. If she did, she would lose her footing in the branches and would never be able to avenge her family. She needed to concentrate. She couldn't let fear and uncertainty consume her. Not now.

Álfara forced negativity from her mind for the best part of the next hour. The closer she got to Stöfnfé, the brighter the sky seemed every time she stuck her head above the tree canopy to check. The darkness that had descended upon the Ljósálfar was anchored in Skógur Hanna Huldu. At least for now. She was getting her bearings now, too, and soon she had found her way to her nest tree.

It looked sadder than usual, as if it too knew of what had happened deeper in the forest and had been waiting to see if Álfara was safe. Álfara hesitated as she made her descent through the tree, stopping at her old lookout nest and then further down at where she and Nikkel had been sitting. For a moment she let her emotions consume her as she thought about how the last emotions she had shared with her family were those of hatred. She didn't hate her brother. She was incapable of hate. Quite the opposite. Now they were gone and she would never get a chance to tell them that she loved them.

A twig snapping below as Álfara perched on the thick branch. Instinctively she drew the gramr from her belt and froze, listening. Had the shadows followed her? Were they here? She couldn't see below very easily from where she was. Cautiously, her heart pounding, Álfara leaned over the edge just enough to see.

It was Nikkel.

She breathed a sigh of relief, sheathed her gramr again and climbed down swiftly. Before she fully knew what she was doing, and without even greeting him, she threw her arms around Nikkel's neck and hugged him tightly.

"Álfara!" Nikkel exclaimed as he stumbled back from the power of her embrace, still holding her to him as he did so. "Are you okay?" He held her at arms length and looked from her tearstained face to the gramr in her belt. It didn't take a genius to realise that she had been through something terrible.

Álfara did not answer. She simply burst into tears and sobbed into her friend's shoulder. Nikkel let her sob, saving his questions for when she was done. He rocked her gently, instinctively, and let her pour out her emotion. Only when, eventually, she stepped back and wiped her eyes did he dare prompt further. Her cheeks were shimmering even more than normal from the tears. Using his sleeve cuff, Nikkel cleaned off her face gently for her and met her watery eyes.

"Okay. Tell me everything." He prompted in a quiet voice.

Álfara swallowed hard and nodded, looking over her shoulder into the forest where hours before she had fled the darkness that consumed all she had ever known. Tucking her curled boots beneath her, Álfara sank down onto the pine needle strewn forest floor and pulled her coat tighter around herself, wondering precisely where to begin. Nikkel mirrored her gesture and sat beside her, his hand firmly wrapped around his friends in a show of comfort. It was pitch dark around them now, the trees whispering quietly far above. Something about the way they were swaying almost seemed to be an embrace, as though they were shielding the friends from outside eyes. Perhaps they knew all that had happened in a few short hours.

Álfara sighed.

"It all started with Aksel." She sniffled, clutching her mittened fingers tightly. Despite her tumultuous relationship with her older brother and his betrayal of her, she had still loved him. It was hard to think that she may never see him again. She forced herself to swallow all emotions connected to her relationship with her family and the heaviness of their loss, and instead focus on the facts of the last few hours. Nikkel only listened, his copper eyes fixed intensely on Álfara's face as she avoided them. She knew looking at her friend would force her to break down again, and she needed to stay strong as she told him everything.

When she got to all she had found in the book her father gave her, however, Nikkel interrupted for the first time. She had not yet told him about the devastation of her people, but Nikkel was not an unintelligent boy. He had a heavy feeling that something awful had happened without needing to be told. Instead, he let his fascination with this secret overweight his need for all of the facts to be spelled out.

"So your father knew all along?"

"That there was some great secret connecting Ljósálfar and Banvænn?" Álfara blinked, grateful that he had asked the question now before she had to relive her father's last moments. "I think so." She swallowed her emotions and fumbled in her satchel. She, like Nikkel, was happy to speak of this now and not after she had inevitably broken down again.

Álfara pulled out the page that she had tucked into her satchel before that awful creature had smashed through her window and ravaged her life. She forced herself to focus on the inked text on the parchment as she held it out to Nikkel. Nikkel took the page reverently and scanned the swirled text in awed silence. He read it more than once as though to allow the information to sink into his mind, then handed it back to Álfara.

"Well." Was all he could manage to say.

"Is that it?" Álfara posted the page back into her bag and scowled at him. "After all of this: the dreams, the darkness attacking my people, and now this? All you can say is 'well'?!"

"What else would you like me to say?" Nikkel asked, his cheeks flushing pink as they often did when he felt any intense emotions. "I've always known I was meant for something more than farming, but I never knew what. When I met you I thought my destiny would manifest then, and it has."

"After a great tragedy." Álfara sniffed angrily. She wasn't angry at Nikkel, far from it. He was her only companion now. She was angry at the way destiny had manifested itself, and the fact he had said out loud what she had been thinking so brazenly, as though he could see through a window into her mind. She, too, had been thinking about the entire event being a sick joke set forth by destiny, and Nikkel speaking the same words aloud only made them more real.

"Yes, of course." Nikkel eyed her warily. The last thing that he wanted to do was offend her. "But you see what I mean? Have you not felt it since we met, Álfara?"

"Felt what?" Álfara said, though she knew exactly what. She avoided his eye just enough to indicate to Nikkel that she was bluffing. She knew exactly, as did he.

"The winds of change pushed us together." Nikkel squeezed her fingers earnestly. She looked at him at last, her expression all that was needed to accept his words. "We were meant to meet, Álfara." He continued, his voice low and solemn and his grip on her fingers tight and wanting. "And in our meeting we seem to have set things in motion."

"We had nothing to do with the rising darkness." Álfara didn't wholly believe her words, but she knew she had to register her complaint all the same.

"No." Nikkel conceded with a small nod. "But we have everything to do with stopping it."

There was a small silence as they looked at one another.

"Don't you see?" Nikkel pushed, although he was fairly sure, judging by Álfara's expression, that she saw all too clearly. "We have both dreamed of the lights of the North, great magical rainbows in the sky that will help to break up the darkness, and your book has proved it. Descendants of Einar, Álfara. You and I. We come from different worlds, races and cultures but together we are the ones to stop the darkness."

"How?" Álfara did not contest his words for she knew them to be true. She had been thinking much the same as she had perched alone in her tree in the hours since the devastating darkness had come a-calling. She knew the lights of the North meant so much more than she knew, and that her father would not have chosen his dying day to tell her this immense secret if it wasn't for a reason. She had a feeling Nikkel was sent to her, and she to him, for a reason beyond breaking down barriers. She just wished it did not all fall to them. She was not old enough to handle the fate of the world, though the world seemed to have made up her mind for her.

"We have to go North, Álfara." Nikkel said determinedly. He pulled his own satchel-strap over his shoulder and climbed to his feet, his grubby boots dislodging the pine-needles that had softened under his weight. "We have to stop the darkness."

Álfara could only nod.

There was no arguing, not now.

7
Chapter Seven
UNLIKELY
COMPANIONS

7 | Unlikely Companions

The energy driven winds of change and adventure blew around them as the unlikely companions, aligned by necessity and a sense of valiancy, set off through Heimur, trekking far away from anyone and anything they had ever known. It was companionable, having each other, joined together for a higher purpose. As they walked, making their way across the völlurs - great meadows filled with flowers that survived in all weathers, and vangurs - fields with great horned matardýr raised to eat - that spanned out from

Stöfnfé and Skógur Hanna Huldu, they talked about their shared visions as though they had not already analysed every second of them.

Never before, at least in Álfara's lifetime, had Ljósálfar ventured outside of the warm, safe bosom of Skógur Hanna Huldu. Not that Álfara knew about, anyway. Certainly not since the war. As a result of her groundbreaking pioneering trek, Álfara's head and pointed ears were on a constant swivel, observant of the unfamiliar world around them and the dangers it might hold. Leaving the forest was more than Álfara could ever have hoped for herself, dreaming as she had so often about adventure and noble deeds. But she was filled with doubts all the same. Was she making the right decision? Were her family alive somewhere back inside the forest? By leaving them behind to the darkness, was she condemning them?

She couldn't think like that. Nikkel was right. They had been brought together for a reason, and they had to move forwards. North. Álfara pushed such thoughts from her mind. All her life she had hoped to make a name for herself, and now, in hopefully discovering a secret to defeating the rising darkness that threatened to smother all those who claimed to be the good of Heimur, Álfara finally felt her life-long wish could come to fruition and, perhaps, the world could be saved all at one.

If she survived, of course.

Nikkel seemed to be thinking something similar as they climbed over the various natural fences that surrounded the open völlurs and vangurs of Heimur, paying as little mind to the resident matardýr as possible in the hopes they too would pay the wanderers no mind. He was not as attuned to the natures of the world as

Álfara was, but he could nevertheless sense a change as they made their way further North. Nikkel did not seem to regret setting out without saying goodbye. His grandfather would never understand, anyway. Of that he was sure.

Nikkel had never been outside of Stöfnfé, except of course for the minute trek he made into Skógur Hanna Huldu to visit Álfara, and he was filled with a great sense of purpose and desire the further out they ventured. His soul was light in spite of the seriousness of the quest upon which they found themselves. He busied himself in times of nervousness by observing the ancient map he had pulled from his grandfather's shelves. What he had not told Álfara the night before, when he had set out from his house for the final time, is that his dream had shown him all that was happening in Skógur Hanna Huldu. He would not tell her, but he had seen the

132

darkness consume her people. He knew, without being told, all that she was going through. He had to stay strong for her as they set along on their path of destiny. That was why he had taken the map before setting out to find his friend.

It wasn't hard to know where they were going, of course, as the Kaltspids rose, enormous and intimidating, on the horizon, their tips forever lost in the gilded clouds of the sky. However, there would undoubtedly be many dangers along the way.

It was common knowledge to anyone living in Heimur that the world was a dangerous place. Even with the Dökkálfar retreating into their caves and hollows, there were many other beings who could and would overpower two small adventurers. Ulfurs, Björnings, even rabid Dvergers should they feel so inclined, would happily eat up a rogue Ljósálfar and a lost Banvænn. The further North they trekked, the more Álfara felt relieved that she had risked taking her father's old gramr from where he had hidden it inside their chimney flue. He had no use for it, after all. It was no help against the darkness that threatened to engulf Skógur Hanna Huldu.

Álfara broke herself out of such thoughts and tightened her grip on her father's gramr. So far, the worst they had seen was a matardýr bull who caught them upwind and surveyed them suspiciously until they left that specific vangur. Though it was big, it didn't seem to view them as too much of a threat. Álfara found herself hoping any creatures they passed would treat them the same as that. Somehow, she doubted it.

The elements seemed to be in their favour, the winds of change that accompanied them were strong. As they settled into the various trees scattered across the landscape each night, the stars shone down on them through the bright night sky, watching over them and keeping them safe. Nikkel was still not very good at climbing trees, but Álfara was a pro and managed to succeed in helping him to at least the lowest branches. They had become very good at strapping themselves onto the branch with the silvered rope Nikkel had brought with them, another last minute acquisition, and they shared the supplies gathered by Álfara companionably before drifting off to sleep. Nikkel, like all Banvænn, often lived on a diet of various meats, but in the presence of the nature-fed Ljósálfar he called his friend, he had taken to a different dietary approach.

Already, as they shared the various nuts, berries and fruits Álfara had packed from Skógur Hanna Huldu, Nikkel felt strangely stronger. He had always been told that eating meat would make him strong, but this diet that Álfara coveted told him otherwise. He found himself not missing meat, and as they walked through the vangurs that held the matardýr he would have eaten quite happily, Nikkel found himself almost apologetic at having consumed their kin. There was one berry, a large beige one which Álfara called 'kexber', that tasted like honeyed flat cakes back home. He found himself wanting to eat all of the kexbers in the pack, but Álfara held back. She almost heard her grandmother's voice as she warned him that they were very sugary and would make him quite round. As Nikkel drifted off to sleep most nights in their various trees, he found himself craving more kexbers, perhaps with a glass of milk, and the thought comforted him well into his fevered dreams.

Although Nikkel and Álfara knew each other quite well from all of those secretive days back in Skógur

Hanna Huldu, their journey across Heimur brought them closer still. Álfara found herself telling Nikkel of her hopes and dreams as a child, digging deeper into them than the superficial information she had told him before. It was true, as she had said, that she wished to explore what Heimur beheld, but now she had disclosed that not only did she seek to explore, but also to unite. It was Álfara's belief, and now Nikkel's too, that Heimur had too long been divided. Without her family to hold her back, Álfara was of the opinion that it was now her destiny.

"Think about it," Álfara had said as they climbed over a natural fence woven by brambles between one völlur and another, "Heimur is splintered. The Banvænn fear the Ljósálfar, the Ljósálfar are constantly watching for Dökkálfar, and in between all of the creatures and lesser-known races, like the Huldi and the Dvergers, fall between the cracks. No wonder they all despise each other, living in their own groups.

"I think the Dvergers enjoy falling between the cracks." Nikkel had chuckled, and Álfara had agreed. The Dverger certainly were secretive, hiding in their rock formations and sacred caves, digging deep into the Earth so as not to have to deal with any other races.

"Well," Álfara had persevered, "what about the Fe? When I was a child my grandmother told me that Fe were responsible for the changes of the seasons, that they were so tiny that we couldn't see them. The Fe and the Ljósálfar share a common ancestor, yet I've never seen or encountered a Fe in my life! Do they even exist anymore?" Álfara asked the question mostly to herself, but Nikkel responded, to her surprise.

"Well, do the seasons still change?" He asked, helping her down from the top of the fence that he had easily scaled.

"I suppose so." Álfara agreed.

"Then the Fe must still exist." Nikkel shrugged, as though it were that simple.

It took just over a week for the trek across the völlurs and vangurs of Heimur to result in Álfara and Nikkel arriving at the outskirts of Norðurtre, the northern forest. They had grown used to keeping to the outskirts of the völlurs and vangurs, creeping through the shadows lest anyone, or anything, spot them out in the open. As luck would have it - or destiny - nothing had paid them mind, and now here they were already in the shadow of the very

Kaltspids that embodied their destination, only the great gossamer fir trees of the Norðurtre standing in their way, towering above them. Álfara was small, but in the presence of these trees she felt positively miniscule. Nikkel seemed to think the same as he reached out, not speaking, and wrapped his gloved fingers around Álfara's hand. Neither of them spoke, but they knew what this meant, and Álfara clutched at Nikkel's hand as he did hers. They had reached Norðurtre, the gateway to the lights of the North and the seat of their quest. It was here that they stopped to take stock.

On the map, Norðurtre looked to be only a fraction larger than Skógur Hanna Huldu. However, in reality, Norðurtre looked as though it might carry on until the edge of the world. In certain circles it was known as the forest of the Gods, and standing in its gossamer shadow it was easy to see why. Unlike the various breeds of trees

140

at home in Skógur Hanna Huldu, which had branches or notches for ease of climbing and treetops that enveloped you like a friendly umbrella in the face of a storm, these dark trees of Norðurtre were pointed and menacing, with straight trunks that stabbed against the sky. Even Álfara felt she would not be able to scale them easily, and if she could not, Nikkel stood no chance.

Nikkel and Álfara exchanged glances, their hands still held for comfort, and both gulped in unison.

"We can turn back, Álfara." Nikkel said in a tone of voice that he forced to appear confident. His face, however, said otherwise. His often rosy cheeks were now bright red as a reflection of his emotion in the moment, and the tip of his nose was glowing to join them.

Álfara considered his words, looking from his face and back up at the enormous trees and the vast blackness of the belly of Norðurtre. She swallowed hard, her mouth dry from either the cold or fear, and her ear points quivered with determination. There was no turning back, and she knew it. Deep down, she was sure Nikkel did too. They had come too far to turn back now, and in that time had convinced themselves that the Heimur was relying on them.

"No we can't." Álfara said defiantly. With her words, she took an assured step into the ingress of Norðurtre. Stealing himself, knowing how close they truly were to their destiny, Nikkel followed her into the shadows of the trees.

Although it was much darker here than in Skógur Hanna Huldu, fundamentally it felt the same. It felt like that feeling you only get from thick forest, the tranquillity, the loneliness, the ancient history trapped within the trunks all around you. The breeze that had accompanied the companions on their journey thus far followed them into Norðurtre, licking their hairs around their faces and tickling their skin. They were no longer holding their hands, but they stuck close together as they ventured into the woods, deeper and deeper. Álfara, who was very in tune with the secrets forests held, did not feel uneasy within Norðurtre, not as much as she thought she would anyway. It wasn't as warm and welcoming as Skógur Hanna Huldu, but it wasn't cold and unfriendly as she had thought it might be. Instead, it felt as though the forest craved their presence within it, as though it had been left alone or had not felt a friendly presence for so long. The trees did not whisper to one another as those at home in Skógur Hanna Huldu did, but they swayed in the winds of change all the same. Underfoot, where in Skógur Hanna Huldu the ground would be littered with leaves and berries, here it was a carpet of pine needles with a sprinkling of snow that had drifted in through the gaps in the fir spearheads. It rarely snowed in Skógur Hanna Huldu, but Álfara knew exactly what it was. The old stories were filled with tales of how once the entire world had been covered in the white water. Álfara found herself yearning to touch it, but she did not want to delay their travel by getting too wrapped up in snow, of all things.

In Skógur, animals could be heard all around, scurrying to and fro and hopping between branches. The trees themselves whispered to one another and invited their residents to join in their conversations. In Norðurtre, however, the only animals Álfara could hear was the occasional caw of a Hvafn high in the treetops. She had never felt welcomed by Hvafn. Though beautiful, with their sleek back bodies and all-seeing eyes, there was an air about them that never failed to remind Álfara

144

of the Dökkálfar from the stories. Now that Álfara had seen a being of darkness up close, she was all the more of the opinion that Hvafn had to share a similar ancestor. The caw of the Hvafn here set her teeth on edge, causing the hair on the back of her neck to prick up and her lips to tremble. She was comforted by the soft footsteps beside her that told her Nikkel was not far away. To its credit, Norðurtre did not feel overly unwelcoming, as long as the Hvafn could be ignored.

Nikkel and Álfara did not know how long they walked in as straight a line as they could manage through Norðurtre, hoping they moved in the direction of the Kaltspids. The lighting was uneasy, with what little sunlight that breached the treetops causing dusty patches on the needle-strewn ground. The wind of change that accompanied them was reassuring, sweeping them along on their way in what they hoped was a Northern direction. They could not directly see the sun, however, so did not know for sure. They also did not know the time of day, nor how long they had been walking deeper and deeper into Norðurtre. Time and being seemed to stop still in this queer place.

They hardly spoke as they walked, just enough to assure the other of their presence, and share affirmations of bravery as it grew ever darker and more dense. Neither of them had expected to get this far without running into some form of foe. She wasn't sure even destiny had a say in this deep forest. It couldn't be destiny alone keeping them from danger.

Álfara found herself wondering if their presence here and the sound of their anxious footsteps was enough to keep the Björnings or dark things at bay. In their anxious state, neither of them succeeded in realising that the Hvafn had stopped cawing long ago.

Álfara felt they had been walking at least two hours, and had come to some form of clearing, when suddenly the air around them no longer felt warm. The winds of change had abandoned them now, sweeping up into the treetops and out of Norðurtre. There was no longer so much as a breeze. Álfara instantly felt the same as she had back home in Skógur Hanna Huldu on that fateful night when the consuming darkness had returned. Instinctively, the Ljósálfar pulled her father's gramr from her belt and held it up in front of her. Nikkel, who was not as attuned with the forces of nature as she, nonetheless sensed something was wrong and held up the roughly hewn staff he had collected along the way in a defensive fashion. Both of them had stopped walking as soon as the wind had left them. As if sharing one mind,

147

they turned so that they were back to back in the small clearing amongst the copse of trees where the air had changed so drastically. If anything was going to creep up on them, at least this way they stood a chance of beating it to it.

The silence was deafening. Álfara turned her eyes skywards to the treetops above them, hoping to catch sight of the beady black eyes of Hvafn looking back at her. Nothing. Nikkel squinted into the dark trees that surrounded them, hoping that the silence had merely come from a Björning or something that may be physically defeated.

Instead, and with a cry of fear, what Nikkel saw barrelling towards them with ease through the forest, was a pack of shadow beasts wielding swords made of bent darkness.

8
Chapter Eight
LEGENDS MADE REAL

8 | Legends Made Real

"Álfara!"

Nikkel barely had time to warn his companion before the shadow creatures were upon them. Álfara, responding to his cry, rolled out from behind him and raised her gramr, connecting instinctively with one of the creature's blades. Up close, these shadows seemed impossible. They shimmered like dark smoke, but they were inherently shaped like a humanoid - solid. As Álfara's gramr connected with the shadow blade of the creature she had targeted, it snarled in an abysmal tongue that made Álfara's skin crawl. Álfara was momentarily stunned by her own instinctive reflexes and by the creature's strength, before she managed to swing her gramr back again and brought it back down upon the creature's blade.

Behind them, Nikkel had raised his rough alder staff in defence of the two creatures that bore down upon him, their blades sinking into the staff but doing nothing to break it. He had whittled it on one chilly night as he had kept watch from their treetop nest, Álfara snoring softly beside him. The staff had fallen in front of him on the branch as though gifted to him, and Nikkel had wasted no time in etching protective runes into its bark. It had been given to him by some higher power, and now it seemed enough to prevent harm coming to him.

Nikkel had been right, he was much stronger than he looked, and he let out a cry of anguish that forced both creatures back. Álfara did not have time to blink at what had happened, but she managed to register that no ordinary Banvænn would have achieved that level of repel. Especially a farm boy. It further cemented their suspicion that she and Nikkel were descendants of Einar himself. Before she could think on it further, Álfara was consumed again into her own combat before she had much time to pay more heed to her companion. Regardless, he seemed able to handle himself against the creatures, whatever they were.

A second creature appeared at Álfara's side, and she found herself fetching up a rotten tree bark that lay at her feet in lieu of a shield. Defending herself against one of the creatures, she fought against the other, her teeth gritted in an attempt to maintain her composure and attune her Ljósálfar reflexes. She was, after all, descended from Einar himself, the greatest Ljósálfar warrior who had ever lived. Had she been forced to fight for her life sooner, she was sure she would have taken to it as naturally as she did now.

Within moments, Álfara had beaten back one of the creatures and used her gramr to stab it into the trunk of a tree. It cried out in pain as her curved silver blade pierced its chest, and as she pulled the gramr back out of its body, it slumped to the ground at her feet. She did not have time to dwell on the murder she had just committed, or the fact that it could feel pain, as another creature came at her from behind. Before she realised it, she had backflipped over it and come round behind it, regaining her footing just in time to cross her gramr with its shadow blade. It was angrier than the first, fuelled by the loss of its companion perhaps, and it did not intend to show Álfara mercy. It engaged her in a furious duel that sent her stepping backwards, her light-footedness coming in more handy than it ever had as she parried every blow.

Nikkel, armed with his alder staff, was not having as much luck as Álfara. No matter how he spun it about his person, though with great expertise, their blades were much stronger. Notches were being hacked out of the staff here and there, and the creatures were relentless, but still it did not break. Just as Álfara found herself with a strong opponent in the sheer anger it held, Nikkel faced the same in the determination of their attack. The creatures beat Nikkel and Álfara back until they were once more back to back. They did not need to look at one another to know that, if they kept on this way, neither of them would survive.

It was then that a sudden light appeared through the trees - silver, bright, like the stars. It was coming at them fast and Álfara did not have much time to wonder if it were friend or foe before it barrelled into them, knocking both Álfara and Nikkel to the ground. It took them both a moment to realise, lying winded on the ground as they did, that the creature had enormous antlers, the source of the light, and was using said antlers to spear the creatures - two of them - and toss them into the trees surrounding them. Álfara and Nikkel, their hands instinctively over their heads for protection, dared peer up at their surroundings in time to see a small being, barely larger than the Banvænn dogs in Stöfnfé, swinging an enormous antler not too unsimilar to those on the head of the light creature. The tiny creature stabbed the antler, which must have been sharpened to a point, into the stomach of the final creature, sending it screaming and writhing to the ground.

Silence fell once more in the clearing, though it was no longer as heavy as before. It took Álfara and Nikkel a moment to dare look up at their saviours fully, lest they not be saviours and instead another foe.

However, they were relieved to see that the small creature, which now upon closer inspection resembled a gnome or sorts, was paying them no mind.

"Nasty blighters, them Myrkur Rogues." Said the gnome-like creature, more to his companion than to Álfara and Nikkel. His companion, now obviously a large glowing reindeer sort of creature, palomino grey in colour with great velveteen antlers donned with leaves and flowers, grunted in response. Álfara's eyes widened as she recognised what it was: a Rensdyr! The Gods had made Rensdyr out of pure starlight, fashioned them as forest guardians, but in the Great War they had all but become extinct. Álfara surveyed the Rensdyr reverently. Never in her wildest dreams had she ever expected to see one in the flesh, let alone one save her from certain death. She felt humbled and terrified all at once.

The gnome, pulling Álfara's focus, began brushing the leaves and branches from his long white beard with his stumpy little fingers. "Unusual for them to come this far North." He put his stubby little hands on his hips and surveyed the bodies of the shadow-beings that now lay limp before them, scattered around the clearing in various states of impalement. "I wonder why that is?"

He seemed entirely oblivious to the existence of Álfara and Nikkel, still laying as they were on their stomachs in the shadows of the trees where they had been knocked. Álfara and Nikkel exchanged looks and then, as one mind, began to rise to their feet. Nikkel took Álfara's hand to help her up, leaning himself on his alder staff. Álfara did not sheathe her gramr, not until she knew for sure that these saviours meant them no harm.

"Sorry," said Nikkel, his voice quavering a little from the shock of it all, "but, what did you say they were?"

The gnome-like creature stopped in the process of now ringing out his tall pointed hat of shadow-being blood, a dripping, stinking black, and turned to face Nikkel and Álfara. He had a pouchy face and bright red cheeks, his large cherry-tomato bulbous nose protruding beneath the brim of his hat when he placed it back atop his grey haired head. "Myrkur." He said plainly, as though Nikkel was stupid for not knowing what 'Myrkur' were. "Don't tell me you've no idea what a Myrkur is, boy?" He laughed a little rudely, though there was a jolly tone to his chagrin. He didn't seem to notice, nor care, that Álfara and Nikkel were not from around here and were clearly different from each other. Though he surveyed them up and down, taking in their travelling clothes and the black Myrkur blood they, too, were covered in, he did not query further about their presence here.

Nikkel looked at Álfara, who shrugged minutely, and then back at the gnome-like man.

"Sorry," He said again, "I haven't a clue."

The gnome-like man blinked his small, black, puffy eyes at Nikkel in amazement. He then looked incredulously at his Rensdyr companion, and then back at Nikkel.

"Shadow-beings?" He asked, still speaking as though this should be obvious. Nikkel and Álfara shook their heads again. "Nightmares?" He tried again. Nikkel and Álfara shrugged. "Crikey, what do they teach kids nowadays? Why venture into Norðurtre and not expect creatures like Myrkurs who thrive on loneliness and despair?" Álfara and Nikkel stayed silent about their lack of education on the matter, Álfara busying herself with sheathing her gramr. It didn't seem like she would need it now. School was not a priority in Stöfnfé, not for farmers, and Ljósálfar did not actually go to school. The gnome sighed. "Myrkur are beings of pure darkness, manipulated and forced into being beyond their will. They're nasty blighters, especially the rogues." He kicked the nearest for good measure. The Rensdyr nodded in agreement. "How can your parents expect you to defend yourself around here if you don't even know what the threat is?" He scoffed and pulled his antler spear out of the nearest corpse beside him, shaking his head so that his beard quivered.

"My parents didn't really tell me anything," Álfara explained, finally getting to her feet and dusting herself down. She turned to help Nikkel up too. She felt a pit in her stomach that she hastened to banish. She couldn't afford to worry about her parents now. She swallowed the heavy, thick knot in her throat that threatened to manifest into tears. She looked at the body of these Myrkur rogues and realises, with a stab in her heart, that these were very similar to the ones who had attacked her home and her people.

Nikkel, sensing her despair, reached out and squeezed her hand.

"We don't have parents." Nikkel said plainly.

The gnome-like creature looked between them, a sudden, genuine, look of remorse on his wrinkled face.

"I do apologise." He said with a small bow that shook his pointed hat. He then narrowed his eyes at them both, noticing as Álfara pulled her own knitted cap back down over her ears. It had fallen off during the battle. "Here," he said in an accusatory tone, pointing his stubby finger at Álfara so that she stepped backwards in alarm. "Are you one of them?"

"One of what?" Álfara asked defensively, her hands clamped tight over her ears in reaction, feeling much like she had when she and Nikkel had first become acquainted.

"Them Ljósálfar?" He looked her up and down, his eyes wide. He took in her pointed boots, green eyes and sage curls, and the slight glittering of her coppered skin. He nodded, smug that he had worked it out.

Álfara glanced at Nikkel for support. He gave her a little shrug that indicated he didn't know what to say. Álfara looked back at the man and nodded. She had, after all, put away her weapon. He did not feel like as much of a threat as the Myrkur, anyway. "I am." She admitted.

"Bit far from home, aren't you?" The gnome asked. "What brings you so far North? Least of all to Norðurtre. It's nothing like Skógur Hanna Huldu, after all?! I thought all Ljósálfar were home-bodies, never venturing far from their front door."

"That's our business." Nikkel said curtly, drawing his red coat back around himself and flexing his Alder staff, making sure it had survived the fight.

The gnome-like creature narrowed his eyes at Nikkel this time and Nikkel stopped shifting his staff.

"You're no elf, however. What are you?" He demanded.

Nikkel looked at the snowy ground, tapping a rock nervously with his toe so as to avoid answering the question. He did not need to, however, as the Rensdyr made a grunting noise that the gnome-like man seemed to understand as though it were words. His eyes widened even more, though still tiny in his round red face.

"A Banvænn...!" He gasped. "You're *definitely* far from home and out of your comfort zone! And you two together? Bit of a strange pairing, isn't it?"

Nikkel's eyes widened in worry, a motion that Álfara noticed. She scowled on Nikkel's behalf and turned to the man.

"What are you, might I ask?" Álfara said in a commanding tone that matched that of their inquisitor.

The gnome-like creature took his suspecting eyes from Nikkel and looked at her. "Don't tell me you don't even know a Nisse when you see one?"

It was Álfara's turn to widen her eyes, though Nikkel continued to look confused.

"A Nisse?" She asked, her tone one of awe in spite of herself. "I thought you were all extinct?!"

"Clearly not, as I'm standing right here." The Nisse said grumpily. "Last time I checked, anyway."

"The legend made real!" Álfara breathed as the Nisse swept his pointed hat from his head and took a long bow that resulted in his large nose almost denting the snow. "Pieni Gardvord," He said proudly, "At your service." He swept his hat back onto his head just as swiftly as he had taken it off.

"What's a Nisse?" Nikkel asked, his question resulting in a scoff from both the Nisse and the Rensdyr.

"What's a Nisse, he says." Pieni nudged the Rensdyr with his elbow and they both laughed, the Rensdyr grunting rhythmically. "A Nisse is me, boy." He said.

"Protectors." Álfara was still in awe of the legendary figure now directly in front of her. She had quite forgotten to be cautious.

"I would have thought you'd know about us," Pieni smiled at her, "Us being from the same ancestor and all."

Álfara smiled at him wanly, significantly warming to the grumpy old man. "Of course." She agreed.

"So you're an elf?" Nikkel looked from Álfara to Pieni and back again, still trying to understand. Álfara knew he was looking for pointed ears on Pieni. Pieni looked as if Nikkel had slapped him. As, without realising it, did Álfara. Nikkel shrank a little under their judgemental eye.

"Not in so many words." Pieni explained. "Yes, we share a common ancestor, but we also share that ancestor with Fe, sprites, brownies..." He spat into the snow to show his disgust. "Us Nisse are far more refined. As are, I'm sure you'll agree given your choice of companionship, boy, Ljósálfar."

"Sorry." Nikkel mumbled, looking at his boots. "I'm still learning all of this."

"So the stories are wrong then?" Álfara asked, "The Nisse and Tomten are not extinct?"

"Far from it, my dear," Pieni had warmed considerably to Álfara, it seemed, as though he were a long lost uncle. "We just like to be solitary, is all. Don't play much part in wars or arguments. Keep ourselves to ourselves... 'cept when Myrkur's enter our realm." He kicked the nearest body again to demonstrate his distaste. "This is Töfrandi, one of the last remaining Rensdyr." He gestured to the great starry beast behind him. The Rensdyr, Töfrandi, nodded his magnificent head in greeting, his bronze antlers trembling.

"I knew it..." Álfara whispered to herself, looking at the great creature. He stood seven feet tall, much taller than any creature in Skögur by far, and almost twice her height.

"You'll probably all judge me harshly, but what is a Rensdyr?" Nikkel asked tentatively.

"Magical creatures," Pieni explained, watching as Töfrandi blinked his large eyes softly at Álfara, gathering the measure of her. Pieni seemed to have had enough of chastising Nikkel. "They were created by the Gods long, long ago, blessed with magical abilities. Us Nisse were empowered to protect and conserve them, but as we have dwindled in population, as have they." Töfrandi hung his head in sadness at Pieni's words, though the creature kept his great eyes on Álfara.

"They were moulded from starlight itself." Álfara explained breathlessly. "Far stronger than any other beast modelled in their image." She shook her head, in awe.

"You are beautiful." She told Töfrandi in a breathless tone, stepping towards him. "I've always wanted to meet a real life Rensdyr…" She pulled off one of her gloves and held up a tentative hand to Töfrandi, indicating that she wished to stroke his majestic muzzle. "May I?" She asked, her voice a trembling breath.

There was a pause, and then Töfrandi nudged her slender fingers with his great velvet nose, emitting a soft grunt from the depths of his nostrils as he did. "I grew up on stories of the Rensdyr… gifted by Freyja herself with the power of magical flight… by Jörð with the ability to shepherd the trees… "

"Powers long since lost, I'm afraid." Pieni stroked Töfrandi's neck as the Rensdyr hung his head a little. "You should have seen him in his prime." There was a reminiscent tone to Pieni's voice as he looked up at

Töfrandi. "Antlers, all the colours of the seasons... blossoms, leaves, branches growing from them. Birds would nest inside them, bees would pollinate from his flowers... At night moonlight would dance off of his back, stars entangling themselves in his antlers." Pieni sighed heavily, mournfully, as Töfrandi nodded in lament. "A distant memory now, isn't it my friend? All he can do is glow, and even then that's only sometimes."

Töfrandi grunted sadly in response.

"Oh..." Álfara sounded worried that she had offended him, "I am sorry..."

Töfrandi nudged her hand again, indicating that it was all alright really, knowing she hadn't meant to offend him. Pieni smiled proudly at the interaction.

"He likes you." Pieni translated, sounding impressed. "That's not easy, is it Töfrandi, my old friend? Slow to trust, aren't you?" Töfrandi nodded his great head. Pieni chuckled, and Álfara giggled in spite of herself.. "I suppose it's a Ljósálfar thing."

Álfara smiled at Töfrandi for a moment, feeling the magic that flowed from him. There was an unexplained quality to the energy flowing from him to her, a bond that was unexplained. He was looking at her with his deep auburn eyes, a depth within them like that she had never seen. Suddenly scared of the power, Álfara withdrew her hand and cleared her throat, stepping backwards.

"Enough about us old relics of legend." Pieni said briskly. "Tell us about you two. Who are you, anyway? A Banvænn and a Ljósálfar... unusual companions."

Álfara pontificated for a moment, placing her glove back over her fingers and carefully placing each in place. Once done, she gestured to Nikkel.

"Well," She started. "This is Nikkel." She said, "And my name is Álfara."

Pieni bowed his head in polite acknowledgement to the direction of Álfara, but his eyes were fixed on Nikkel. Álfara frowned slightly as she noticed just how intently Pieni looked to her companion.

"Nikkel?" Pieni looked at him as Nikkel bowed his head politely in greeting. "*He who is like God.*" He translated. Nikkel's eyes widened, whilst in contrast Álfara frowned at Pieni, surprised that he should know the meaning of Nikkel's name so readily when Nikkel did not know himself.

"You are both far too far from home." Pieni continued, turning to Töfrandi and shifting the blanket on the Rensdyr's back. He seemed to be preparing them to leave.

"Wait..." Álfara stepped forwards before she really thought about the motion. Pieni turned his head to look at her, his long white beard brushing the tips of his boots. "I'm sure you know the North better than anyone..." She tried to look as pleading as possible whilst still maintaining her dignity, "Perhaps you could help us?"

"That all depends on what you need help with, child." Pieni said with a well-worn suspicious glint to his eye, turning his attention fully back to them. "A Nisse should not refuse the help of those who ask without just cause."

"We're trying to get to Hásætishöll." Álfara explained. She felt a great sight different now about Pieni and Töfrandi then she had moments earlier. Something about the once grumpy Nisse was now warm and welcoming. The old Nisse, however, looked at her in fear and alarm, an expression matched by his Rensdyr companion. His face made her feel she had been wrong to speak out plainly.

"Why on Earth would you want to do that?" Pieni asked accusatively, in a dark tone of voice. "Nothing there but trouble, girl."

There was a momentary silence that echoed endlessly around the forest clearing. The snow littering the ground and falling softly on the bodies of the Myrkur did little to aid the lack of sound, adding an all-in-all depth to the silence. Nikkel looked at Álfara, and she back at him, both of them trying to decide what to say. Then, when they could stand the silence no longer, Nikkel cleared his throat and looked Pieni in the eye.

"The darkness is rising in the South." He said darkly.

"That is all too clear." Pieni grunted, gesturing at the Myrkur. "Let me rephrase my question. What are you two children, Ljósálfar or not, doing looking for Hásætishöll? There is nothing there for you both but trouble, or even death. Go home where it is safe... at least for now."

"But it isn't." Álfara said sadly. Pieni narrowed his eyes at her, sensing the heavy sadness in her tone. "They came to my home, Pieni. These... Myrkur. They killed my people. My family..." Her voice broke as tears spurted uncontrollably down her cheeks. Nikkel squeezed her hand reassuringly. Pieni shifted from one foot to the other, awkward. Töfrandi, however, nudged Álfara's arm as though he understood.

"We have to stop them." Nikkel added forcefully. Töfrandi grunted knowingly. Pieni frowned at the

Rensdyr as though he understood. He seemed to be dithering.

There was a long silence.

"Please, Pieni..." Álfara pleaded, taking an instinctive step towards him. "If these Myrkur are not far from Dökkálfar kind, then the future of Ljósálfar and Banvænn, and perhaps Heimur, rests on us finding Hásætishöll." Her emerald eyes shone brightly as she begged him, her gloved hand wiping her tears. "Please."

Pieni's stern eyes softened as he looked between them. Behind him, Töfrandi made another small grunting sound that could have been encouragement, but it could also have been disgust. Pieni glanced at the beast and then looked back at them.

"You're just children. How do you know of Hásætishöll at all? Especially you, Nikkel... this is not of your world. The Banvænn made that perfectly clear when they retreated from the wars around them. Why even leave the safety, the blissful ignorance, of your people?" He shook his head in a judgemental manner, his tone of voice one laced with concern rather than disdain.

Álfara glanced at Nikkel, who in turn glanced back at her. He swallowed hard, his mouth dry, and turned back to Pieni. Álfara seemed to trust them, or at the very least she seemed to not see them as a threat. Perhaps now was the right time to tell Pieni all. Perhaps, as Álfara seemed to think, Pieni and Töfrandi really could help them. Nikkel cleared his throat again and opened his mouth. "I have had dreams of it. We both have. The dreams tell me it's the answer." He said quietly. Despite their soft tone, however, these words caught Pieni's attention, and the bells on Töfrandi's antlers quivered as his ears twitched in alertful response.

"Dreams?" Pieni replied, looking from Álfara to Nikkel, then taking a few long strides, his beard and robes creating a track in the fresh snow, towards Nikkel. He was much, much smaller than the well-built boy, but something about his attitude made Nikkel shrink a little under his gaze. "What kind of dreams, lad?"

Nikkel looked at Álfara for help, not knowing what to say now. She gave him a little shrug in response, one that told him he should speak plainly.

"Well," He started in a small voice, "There's a hall... a great stone hall with a vast domed ceiling. There are three thrones in the hall, and the ground is covered in snow as though there is no ceiling at all. The sky is filled with rainbow lights that dance."

"That's all." Álfara added, but something in Nikkel's expression caused her to frown. "Isn't it?"

"There's more, isn't there?" Pieni asked.

Álfara frowned further as Nikkel cautiously nodded. He was avoiding looking at Álfara. He had never told her of any more to the dream. She had certainly never dreamed of more. Perhaps that was why Nikkel had kept it quiet. Álfara felt a little betrayed, but she could not interrupt now. Pieni was staring at Nikkel so intently she felt it was not her place.

"What are you doing in this dream?" Pieni demanded, causing Nikkel to shrink back a little more.

"Walking in." Nikkel stammered in response. He did not look at Álfara, though she continued to stare at him.

"Just walking in... and then I stand in the middle, in front of those thrones."

"Is there anything in the thrones? Anyone?" Pieni continued. The tip of his hat only just reached Nikkel's nose, but Nikkel was trembling with fear of the small creature. He shook his head.

"How do you know it is the answer?" Pieni continued. Nikkel, at last, looked to Álfara for help. Álfara shrugged again, feeling helpless in the moment as her friend seemed to need her in spite of all he had kept from her.

"I hear a voice." Nikkel replied in a hurried tone of voice, shrinking ever further beneath Pieni's authority. "A voice telling me to go to Hásætishöll. It says I will find the answer there. The way to defeat the darkness." He blinked hard. "But it says I will need help... the help of a Ljósálfar, to be precise.."

For the first time Álfara truly understood why Nikkel had been venturing into Skógur Hanna Huldu, how they had even met to begin with. Why had he never told her?

"It's why Nikkel brought me with him, Pieni." Álfara realised. "I was the first Ljósálfar he came across who did not run away from him." It all made sense now. She wasn't sure if it was destiny or not, but it felt right to say so. Something had pulled them together, descendants of Einar or not. She wasn't even angry at Nikkel for keeping these details from her. "I believe his dreams are really the answer."

Pieni's head snapped to her now, his small eyes black with intensity. Álfara did not shrink under his scrutiny, but instead held her ground. After looking her up and down a few times, seemingly trying to work out his next move, Pieni's head snapped back to Nikkel.

"You dream this often, boy?" He asked. There was now a different tone to his voice, a softer tone. It sounded almost like concern.

Nikkel nodded hastily. "Almost every night." He said. "It didn't mean much to me at the start, I put them down to my own imagination... but then I saw Álfara and we began talking and..." His voice tailed away. Pieni had turned away from him, pacing as best he could now in the thickening snow. He was muttering to himself under his breath in a language neither Álfara nor Nikkel knew, but one that Töfrandi seemed to understand. The Rensdyr nodded along to whatever it was Pieni was muttering. Álfara caught one word that did not translate from the common tongue: *destiny*. Álfara looked towards Nikkel to see if he understood, but he shook her head at her. Álfara instead offered him a small smile, commending him for his bravery in the matter and reassuring him that she understood why he had not told her everything. Nikkel managed a small smile back at her before Pieni turned on his heel, his beard and hat quivering in time.

"We will take you to Hásætishöll." Pieni said, his hands behind his back in a business-like manner as he looked between them. "You cannot make such a journey alone. Especially not if there are more Myrkur out there. If you are right and you are meant to go to Hásætishöll," Pieni peered under his hat brim at Nikkel, the determinedly stern expression back, "then I will personally ensure you do."

Álfara and Nikkel looked at one another, unbelieving smiles upon their lips, and then back at Pieni.

"Thank you, sir." Álfara said. "We will forever be grateful to you."

"Álfara is right, Pieni." Nikkel added eagerly. "When we make it to Hásætishöll and discover why my dreams have been plaguing me, or why we were pulled together, you shall have whatever you both desire in thanks."

It was Pieni and Tofrandi's turn to exchange looks.

"Let's just make it to Hásætishöll in one piece first, shall we?" Pieni grunted, striding to Tofrandi's side. In a series of effortless moves, Pieni used the thick copper fur and the blanket on Tofrandi's back to clamber up to his perch atop of the magnificent beast. "You'll forgive me for riding," He said in an uncharacteristically jovial tone of voice, "But I do have rather little legs."

"We've made it this far on foot," Álfara smiled at Pieni, "We can make it the rest of the way."

She took her pack from Nikkel as he took them both up, drawing her green coat tighter around herself and pulling her fur-lined hat further down upon her head. When they were both ready, Nikkel gave Álfara a nod and then they both looked up at Pieni astride Tofrandi.

"Take us to Hásætishöll, sirs." Nikkel commanded. He did not let his voice quiver, but as they set off walking Álfara could see his legs shaking. There was to be absolutely no turning back now, and both of them knew it. Álfara felt she should prompt Nikkel further about all he had hidden from her, but now did not seem the time. She hoped they would be able to talk about it before much longer.

If only she knew.

9
Chapter Nine
DREAMS OF DESTINY

9 | Dreams of Destiny

$\mathcal{D}$arkness.

Nothing but darkness for all the eye could see.

It was freezing cold. Every pore in Álfara's shining skin screamed with the ice that threatened to encrust her every fibre. The air around her was heavy with a despair that emanated from every inch of the darkness. She could not even see the cloud of frozen breath in front of her for the frosty shadows surrounding her. Álfara opened her mouth to speak but her voice itself seemed to have frozen. She could not move for the ice embedding her feet into the murky ground. She had never felt so lonely in her life.

All around her she heard whispers. They were ancient and evil, nothing like the whispers of the trees back home in Skógur Hanna Huldu.

Home.

Álfara would never see it again. She knew without being told that she would never leave this place. The darkness engulfed her, swallowed her, held her fast in its icy depths. She would never see the light again.

"Álfara".

The darkness whispered to her now, gripping at her skin with its slippery grasp.

"Álfara!"

There was an urgency to its words. Álfara wanted to shut her eyes and succumb to the command of the blackness. What was the point of carrying on with no hope?

"Álfara!"

Álfara blinked her eyes open and found herself bathed in the dawn light shining through the treetops above her. It took her a moment to get a grip of her surroundings. She wasn't lost to the darkness, not even close. It was morning and she was looking up at the canopy of Norðurtre forest. Of course she was.

Álfara sat up and rubbed her sore eyes. Nikkel, her dear friend, was sitting beside her with a concerned expression on his face. He was holding some kexbar close to his mouth but seemed to be unable to finish the motion as he looked at her in concern.

"Are you alright?" He asked. "We heard you moaning in despair." His voice was thick with worry.

Álfara looked over to where she could now see the concerned expressions on Pieni and Töfrandi's faces. They were lying by what was left of their fire, Pieni leaning against the great flank of his Rensdyr companion, his beard twitching with concern and agitation. Álfara pulled her hat comfortingly about her ears and took a moment to soak up the homely feel of the fur-lining, before forcing herself to smile and bask in the light of reality. She wanted nothing more than to forget the darkness of her dream, at least. The lost hope of it all.

"Yes. It was just a dream." She said with a determined nod.

"Of what?" Pieni asked in his gruff voice. "The darkness again?" His tone was all at once concerned and accusatory.

Álfara swallowed. During the two days it had taken them to trek across Norðurtre she had filled Pieni in on her own dreams of the darkness and the lights in the North, much as Nikkel had done. He had listened with as much interest as he had listened to Nikkel, and declared them both children of destiny as though he knew that to be true. Álfara nodded.

"It was everywhere and everything. I couldn't move in it." She said solemnly.

"No light at all?" Nikkel asked in a tone that told Álfara he knew exactly how it felt. She met his eye and shook her head. He lowered his own, telling her all she needed to know. He had seen it too. He knew the feeling of despair of which she spoke.

"I don't know what to tell you, kids." Pieni said as he got to his feet with a groan, throwing water on the fire to extinguish it. It hissed softly and then instantly froze in the cold northern winds. "It's only going to get worse the further North you go."

"Why is that?" Nikkel asked. He shrugged off his own thick red coat and placed it around Álfara's shivering shoulders. She smiled at him in acknowledgment. The warmth began to fill her from the outside in, but the memory of the icy darkness was still gripping her soul deep inside.

"The North used to be Dökkálfar territory, obviously." Pieni grunted as though it were obvious. Nikkel and Álfara exchanged glances. The nisse was tugging on his stout boots in a haste that Álfara's stomach drop. What did he know? "Long ago, in ancient times, but nonetheless. There is a darkness here. A cold." He saw them both staring at him with wide eyes. "You didn't think this would be easy, did you?" He had a mocking smile as he shook his head pityingly at them.

"Nothing worth doing is ever easy." Nikkel responded in a wise voice far beyond his years. "That's what my Grandpa always says."

Álfara couldn't help but smile at him. She had once greatly underestimated the entire Banvænn race. She, like her entire people, had put them down as cowards. Nikkel was single-handedly, and perhaps unknowingly, rewriting the understood history of his entire species. Once this adventure was over Álfara was sure he would go on to do great things.

If they survived it, that was.

Álfara shivered. It wasn't from cold. Inside Nikkel's coat, even the icy darkness wrapped around her heart was thawing. She shivered from something else. Not fear exactly, but something adjacent. Anticipation? A sense of not-knowing? Whatever it was she didn't like it.

"Should we get going?" Álfara asked as she watched Pieni jerk his pack back onto Töfrandi's flank.

"Well, we're not going to save the world sitting here." Pieni replied in his gruff tone. He hitched himself up onto Töfrandi's back and the great Rensdyr climbed steadily to his hooves, looking at Nikkel and Álfara expectantly. For the hundredth time, Nikkel and Álfara exchanged wondering looks. They had come to know each other so well in such a short period of time that these looks spoke volumes.

Nikkel got to his feet and held his hand out to help Álfara up. She still had his coat draped around her shoulders, trailing a little in the light dusting of snow on the ground. Nikkel was taller than her, and growing taller the further they adventured. It had not gone unnoticed by the young Ljósálfar. Right before her eyes her companion was growing from boy to man. His coat swamped her greatly and, as though suddenly self-conscious of it, she held it back out to him. He took it and accepted the small nod she gave him in acknowledgement, returning it with a smile. His face was even growing broader now she looked at it in the dawning light.

Álfara wondered whether this quest was changing her too. She felt much the same: still petite in build and short in height, still slight and light-footed, but perhaps her features were growing wiser just as Nikkel's were. She hadn't seen herself in weeks now.

The Norðurtre seemed to stretch on endlessly. She couldn't quite recall how long it had been since they had entered the thick woodland and encountered Pieni and Töfrandi. It could have been hours; it could have been months. Time seemed to stop still in this dark and ancient forest. One thing was for sure, however. Her dreams were getting darker the closer they got to Hásætishöll, It was as though they were changing in order to match the world around them. From the twitching and muttering she often heard from Nikkel throughout the night, she was sure his dreams were growing darker too. If this had once been Dökkálfar territory then everything seemed to make sense now. There was a heavy gloom that lay over the entire place. Álfara glanced around her anxiously as they began to walk on from their small camp. She felt as though Kollungr himself may be lurking behind the nearest tree.

Pieni appeared to sense the nervousness in her demeanour. He slowed Töfrandi's pace so as to keep in time with Álfara and Nikkel on foot.

"What are you expecting to find once we reach Hásætishöll?" He asked. "If your dreams are bad, I can guarantee you that reality will be twice as much."

"We are aware." Nikkel replied. He was keeping half a weary eye on Álfara to his side. "We're prepared."

Pieni sniffed disapprovingly. There was something about this motion that caused Álfara to frown at him.

"Have you been before, Pieni?" She asked. The words spilled from her mouth before she knew what she was saying.

Töfrandi stopped abruptly as Pieni turned to face her.

"What makes you ask that?" He demanded. Nikkel looked between them, physically shrinking away from the tiny Nisse and his tone.

"Something about the way you hold yourself. The way you talk about it... it's like it's from memory." Álfara asked.

Pieni slid from Töfrandi's back and stalked over to Álfara. He only came up to her nose but she stepped backwards in alarm anyway.

"If you must know," He started, his beard twitching in anger, "I have."

"You have?" Nikkel couldn't stop himself from asking. "When?"

"Why?" Álfara asked in unison with Nikkel's question.

"I once went to the guardians to appeal for guidance."
He was looking Álfara directly in the eyes. For the first
time that she had seen, his own eyes seemed to swim
with tears. "It wasn't just the three master races who got
caught up in the war." He looked to Nikkel. Behind them,
Töfrandi hung his head. He clearly knew the story
already. "It was us small folk too. The minor races. The
one who keep things running." Pieni pulled on his beard
fretfully. Töfrandi stepped over to his friend and nudged
his elbow in comfort. Pieni stroked his antlers in thanks,
and Álfara wondered if Töfrandi felt the same way.
"Kollungr and Einar were so caught up in their own war,
and the Banvænn too cowardly behind their walls, that
they didn't notice us little folk being trampled." Pieni
swallowed hard. "I had dreams once too. The lights of the
North. The hall of stone..." He looked between Nikkel and
Álfara. "The Gods were telling me to find Hásætishöll. To

ask the guardians. So I did." Pieni wiped his nose with the back of his hand and cleared his throat. He clearly did not want to reveal himself to have emotions of any sort. On the contrary, it made Álfara warm to him more.

"What did they say?" Nikkel asked.

"I don't ruddy know." Pieni suddenly lost his emotional demeanour and resumed his grumpy guise, sniffing with contempt. "I never made it past the gates."

Álfara and Nikkel exchanged a look of fear.

"Why not?" Álfara asked, her voice tight in her throat. "Would they not see you?"

"No." Pieni turned from Álfara and set about climbing back onto Töfrandi's expectant back. "I was of little importance."

"How can that be?" Nikkel demanded, his cheeks and nose flushing as they often did when he grew emotional. "They sent you the dreams, didn't they?"

"Someone did." Pieni said darkly, looking around him at the trees. It was as though he expected something dark to jump out right that moment.

Álfara gulped. She felt Nikkel tense beside her.

"It'll be different this time." She said determinedly. "It has to be."

Pieni looked at her. He looked at her for a long time. It was as though he were trying to really read her. She shrank under his gaze and cleared her throat. Pieni sniffed again and turned his attention from her.

"You'll see." He said, spurring Töfrandi forwards. Álfara looked at Nikkel, who shrugged slightly in response. It was clear that neither of them truly understood Pieni, nor would they anytime soon.

The companions trudged along through the Norðurtre. With each step the air grew colder and the sky darker. It was obvious to Álfara and Nikkel that this had once been home of the Dökkálfar. They didn't know how they hadn't seen it before. From the gnarled trees to the dark spears above, it was clear. Álfara found herself wondering whether it still was home to dark forces. Although she remembered what Pieni had said about the Myrkur rogues. He had asked why they would venture so far north, and now Álfara found herself wondering the same. The Myrkur were not Dökkálfar, but they were adjacent kin. The Myrkur, Pieni had explained, had spawned from the darkness just as the Dökkálfar, but where the Gods gave Dökkálfar brains they gave Myrkur ferocity. As a result the Dökkálfar used them as pawns and, during the war, would send them into battle first. Pieni had blown past this fact as though it were not significant, but Álfara could not help but wonder. It was Myrkur, she now realised, that had attacked her home. Now they had attacked Nikkel and herself further north. Were they tracking them? It couldn't possibly be a coincidence, surely? Had the Dökkálfar sent the Myrkur to prevent them from finding Hásætishöll?

What of the dreams of darkness?

After another day of walking through the deepening woods, Álfara found herself unable to fall asleep again. There was too much at stake, she felt. She couldn't risk dreaming of that dark cold again. Not when it had such a physical effect on her. What if it were the Dökkálfar getting inside her mind? She would not let them in. She would stay up all night and watch over them in the deep darkness that crept in so quickly. Days were so short here. Even the night sky filled with stars did not dare peep through the trees of Norðurtre. As Álfara settled herself against a tree trunk in order to watch over her companions, she wondered if they would ever see the lights of the North whether they were there or not. How would they know the way to Hásætishöll without them? She hoped Pieni remembered after all these years.

Nikkel had claimed he would stay awake with Álfara to keep her company in her vigil. She had told him to stop being silly, however, and told him to sleep. He was Banvænn after all. He wasn't as resilient as Álfara. As he had tried to argue this point he had yawned and been forced to give in. He slept now beside Álfara against the trunk. Álfara watched him as he sank from light sleep to deep.

Then the twitching began.

She knew without being told that he was dreaming a similar dream to that she had dreamed. Her heart pounded as she watched him thrash before her, growing more and more determined in his throws. She put a hand on his shoulder in an attempt to comfort him, but she knew he couldn't feel her. Not where he was. She tried to touch his hand, to squeeze it, but as soon as her flesh touched his she recoiled with a gasp. He was ice cold. Colder, if possible.

"Nikkel!" She shouted, panic rising inside her like fog. She gave him a little shake, then a harder shake.

"What's going on?" Pieni asked, woken suddenly from his own slumber. Töfrandi looked over in concern.

"It's Nikkel." Álfara was still shaking her friend. "He's so cold, and he's dreaming…"

Quick as a flash Pieni was by their side, his hat left somewhere where he had been sleeping. His white-whiskered head looked a little naked and bald without it. Álfara couldn't notice much more about his appearance now. Nikkel was the priority.

"Wake up, boy!" Pieni thumped Nikkel on the chest. "Come back to us!"

It didn't work. Nor did Álfara's frantic shakes. It was only when Töfrandi laid his antler cautiously over Nikkel's sleeping form, a shimmering light sparkling through them and into Nikkel, that he woke.

Nikkel's eyes flew open with a gasp and he sat bolt upright, almost knocking Pieni to the ground.

"Nikkel!" Álfara cried with relief, throwing her arms around him in spite of herself. He hugged her back for a moment and then frowned at them all. He was looking as though it were vacant behind his eyes.

"Speak." Pieni ordered, his fingers scratching Töfrandi's fur in thanks for his actions.

Nikkel coughed, his breath causing a small cloud to erupt through his gloved fingers. He seemed to be struggling to speak. When he did, his words came out in a croak.

"It was him." Nikkel said. "Kollungr."

There was silence as they stared at him. The very name hung in the air like dead weight, tied up with all that had ever been dark and evil in Heimur. It was Pieni who spoke first, his tone laced with anger and warning.

"What?!"

Nikkel could sense the danger in what it was he had to convey. Yet convey it he must. They had to know.

"He said he was waiting for me."

Further glances were exchanged, with Álfara looking to Pieni for guidance on how she should be feeling. She knew the sound of Kollungr's name spoken aloud gave her a sinking in her stomach that was greatly uncomfortable. Above all else, however, she was filled with concern for her friend. She frowned at Nikkel. Sweat was standing out on his brow in the dim light. She reached out softly to touch his shoulder, letting him know she was there and she was not angered as Pieni was.

"Where? Hásætishöll?" She whispered. Nikkel shook his head.

"No. In the Ríki Næturinnar." He said in a dark voice.

The heavy silence turned to a silence of confusion. There was no such place, especially not now. Translated from old Alfar, 'Ríki Næturinnar' meant 'Realm of Night' in the common tongue. It was once said this was where Kollungr had been born, and where he had brooded for so long that his hatred and dark thoughts permeated the very air of the place. If such a place even existed. Given Nikkel's dream it seemed it might.

"What does that mean?" Álfara looked at Pieni for guidance. Pieni, however, was glowering darkly at Nikkel. His eyes were almost black with the weight of his thoughts. Álfara swallowed uncomfortably. "I mean... it was just a dream? Surely. He was defeated."

"No." Pieni shook his head. "There is no such thing as dreams where the Dökkálfar are concerned. They control dreams, mould them. He planted that meeting in Nikkel's head."

A tainted, shocked silence followed his words.

Álfara stared from Nikkel to Pieni with wide eyes. What did he mean in saying Kollungr had planted it? Kollungr was dead... wasn't he?

With a pang in her heart, Álfara remembered a legend. When Einar had defeated Kollungr on the field of battle it was said that a shadow left the Dökkálfar's body and fled to the south. It was said to reside in the dark places, the depths of the soul. *Ríki Næturinnar.*

Was Kollungr still out there?

It was a long time before anyone spoke. It was Pieni who broke the silence, fixing Álfara's gaze with a look of acknowledgement. When he spoke, it was in a voice laced with warning. Álfara gripped Nikkel's arm tightly, and he felt for her hand as they watched the Nisse exchange looks with Töfrandi, then take a deep breath as though what he had to say would be hard to hear.

"It means you're in danger." He looked between them. "It means there is likely to be another war, especially if Kollungr It means your destiny is sealed, boy. And yours along with him, Álfara."

Further silence. It was suffocatingly weighty.

"What should we do?" Nikkel whispered.

Pieni drew himself up to his full height. "We need to speak with the guardians. They're the only ones who can help us now."

"Then what are we waiting for?" Álfara said, her voice unwavering and her body filling with resolve. She climbed to her feet and pulled Nikkel up beside her. Töfrandi nudged him softly, allowing him to lean against the Rensdyr in his weakened state of shock. As soon as he did, Töfrandi manipulated his antlers gently to lift Nikkel onto his back. It was clear Nikkel would not be able to walk far, not when his legs were shaking as they were. Pieni nodded in agreement and picked up his hat.

"I agree." He said, tucking it around his ears and then tying his long beard in a knot so that he wouldn't trip over it. "Let's go." He set off at a rapid pace for such a stout creature. "Hásætishöll here we come."

10
Chapter Ten
AS IT WAS TOLD

10 | As It Was Told

*H*ásætishöll was far more imposing than Álfara or Nikkel could or would ever have thought.

By the time the companions had made it through the remainder of Norðurtre, thankfully unharmed, they were exhausted and overwhelmed by the trek. The sight of the great black stone ahead of them was almost too much for them to handle.

"Nikkel..." Álfara whispered in a fearful voice, reaching out and up to her side and gripping Nikkel's hand from where he sat atop Töfrandi with her mittened one, her father's gramr clutched tight in her other hand.

"I know." Nikkel whispered back, his own other hand wrapping around Töfrandi's glimmering mane as though he sought to ground himself.

For a moment they all stood in oppressed silence, simply staring.

The stone fortress was set into the base of the Kaltspids and looked to be made of many, many separate black rocks. Ahead of them were two enormous black stone gates with no handles. The walls were so tall that it hurt Álfara and Nikkel to look up at them, let alone tiny Pieni. The fortress was every bit as ancient as the mountains into which it had been built, and the very stone seemed to whisper as they looked upon it. It oozed an energy that was unexplainable - ancient, sacred, dark.

Even Pieni, who had seen the dark stone before, twitched nervously. His eyes flashed with fear and he reached out from the other side of Töfrandi to grip the Rensdyr's leg. Töfrandi let out a soft-snort in comfort to his companions, his breath causing a small cloud before his nostrils as he did so.

"It's just as I remembered." Pieni muttered, more to himself than anyone else. Töfrandi grunted again.

"Same here." Nikkel said. Álfara and Pieni looked at him. They knew he had never been here physically, but it was obvious from the boy's tone that he was speaking of the dreams that had plagued him since he was a young boy.

"Where are the lights?" Álfara looked up at the darkening sky above the black stone fortress as though the lights of the North would simply erupt before them.

"Long gone." Pieni replied darkly. He was plaiting his long beard now as though preparing for something he would not speak of.

"Pieni…?" Álfara asked worriedly, but a small shake of his head bid her to be silent and not to ask questions.

"I dreamed of the darkness that I knew this place would boast," Nikkel had slid from Töfrandi's back before any of them could argue with him. He walked forwards in his red velvet boots, each step crunching on the ice and snow that lay thickly before them on the ground as he ventured closer to the fortress. "I just never thought it would feel so…" He stopped in his tracks and frowned. The word had evaded him.

"Lonesome." Álfara finished for him. She had been here too, in her dreams, and she knew exactly what Nikkel meant.

"Well," Pieni cleared his throat and mounted Töfrandi's back now that it had been vacated by Nikkel. "There's no point hanging around out here. If you wish to speak with the Guardians, then inside we must go."

"You don't have to come." Nikkel turned to look at Pieni and shook his head. Pieni responded with an indignant snort.

"Of course I do." He spurred Töfrandi forwards so that they were level with Nikkel, Álfara only a few steps behind. "I didn't bring you all this way just to abandon you..."

"But..." Álfara started, remembering Pieni's story of the last time he had ventured close to Hásætishöll and all that had happened to him. He shot her a warning look.

"Do not offend my pride, Álfara." He said in a dangerous tone. Töfrandi grunted in agreement so that Álfara felt herself unable to argue further. "I said I would bring you to the guardians, and bring you to them I shall." He turned to look at Nikkel, who's copper eyes had not moved from the great black stone gate before them. "Come, boy. Inside we must go."

Pieni spurned Töfrandi to walk forwards. Nikkel followed at a shuffle as though pulled along by invisible rope. It was Álfara who hung back as the great stone gate opened magically without touch, as though it could sense them wanting to enter. She watched Pieni, Töfrandi and Nikkel falter as the door creaked open, but it was not enough to stop them from advancing. They continued determinedly, yet Álfara stood where she was. She was stepping from one foot to the other in uncomfortable fear.

Álfara had never been one to feel scared. Not really. Not when the Banvænn had attacked her brother; not when she had found herself lost as a young Ljósálfar. The only time she had felt real fear was when faced with the Myrkur who had attacked her home and killed her family. That was real fear. It permeated her bones and made her shake with a strange cold that could not be pushed away. It was this fear she felt now as she watched her companions approach the gates. There was a darkness to this fear. Something she couldn't place... then...

"Wait!" She cried, stepping forwards to stop them as Nikkel set his first foot inside the black stone doorway. Her shout fell on deaf ears as, all at once, everything went wrong.

All of a sudden there was the sound of moving stones - crash against crash. It was loud enough to be a rock-slide or avalanche from the Kaltspids high above them. Álfara instinctively put her hands over her head as they grew louder and more aggressive all in a split-second, gaining upon them with vigour and terror. In stepping through the gateway, Nikkel seemed to have triggered an invisible forcefield to cause the very walls to move in on them. Pieni was knocked from his steed by a boulder crashing from the top of the fortress wall. Álfara hurried to him, dodging plummeting stones herself as she did so. He was unconscious underneath the boulder and would not rowse even when Álfara shook him. In desperation, the deafening sound of rubble clanging all around her, Álfara looked up to find Nikkel. He was cowering himself, not too far from her, as boulder upon boulder seemed to be moving towards him down the walls of the fortress.

It was then that Álfara realised. They weren't boulders. They weren't even rocks.

She remembered all-at-once the stories she had heard as a child of the unforgiving, foreboding and selfish creatures who dwelled in the mountains. These mountains. These creatures...

"Huldi!" She shouted in warning, when she felt an enormous weight crack the back of her head and all went black.

"Look at this one? Belongs to her. She's only a little thing. So dainty - like she could snap."

Álfara's eyelashes fluttered open in alarm at the sound of the gruff voice. She squinted in the bright blue light that now surrounded her. It took her a moment to get her bearings. She was sitting on a frosty, stone floor that iced right through her trousers. Her knees were bent in front of her and her ankles appeared to be tied together. A wriggle of her shoulders and she realised her hands were tied too, behind her back. Judging by the biting wind swirling around her pointed ears she had been relieved of her hat. She blinked again and tried to focus her blurred eyes on what she could see, turning her head this way and that in spite of the pounding she felt in her ears from the blow to her skull.

Nikkel was sitting to her side, his head lolled in a way that told her he, too, was unconscious. He was tied at the ankles and wrists just as she was, and his hat had also been removed. Álfara wondered if this detail was so their captors could determine race and therefore friend or foe. With a pang to her stomach, she realised Nikkel would be foe to most magical races in Heimur simply because of his rounded ears. He had been born a Banvænn and that meant he was a threat. Álfara struggled harder against the restraints on her wrists, to no avail.

"Keep still."

To her other side Álfara realised Pieni was bundled in a ball and bound entirely, with the ropes tying his ankles to his wrists. Whoever their captors were obviously viewed Nisse as a threat. They weren't going to take any chances, that was for sure.

"Keep still." Pieni urged again. He had his eyes closed and his words emitted as a hiss from the side of his mouth, his lips barely moving. Álfara did as she was told and sat still, keeping her head down in case anyone was watching and determined her state of alertness to be a threat. Through her eyelashes she continued to survey the scene.

They were trussed up against a wall in a bright, frozen room. Frost lined the floors and walls and ice hung from the black stone ceiling, the light from a small hole in the roof enough to cast blue shadows upon them all. With another pang to her heart, Álfara's eyes scanned upwards and she realised Töfrandi was strung upside down from a beam across the ceiling. His hooves were tied together around the beam and he was hanging mournfully upside down, his long neck outstretched from the weight of his great antlers. His eyes met hers sadly and he moaned mournfully, his warm breath creating a small cloud in the cold room. She tried to look at him with a look of promise, but he didn't seem able to see it.

Ahead of them, at the other side of the room, were two hulking great stone-men who were holding up various items of their captive's belongings as though inspecting them for weaponry - or value. They were instantly recognisable as Huldi, and Álfara felt her breath catch in her chest with fear. They were far bigger and more dominating than any myth she could ever have been told. Standing at least six and a half feet in height, far taller than Álfara or Nikkel, and they seemed to stretch the same length to either side. The little she could see of their faces told her that the Huldi were every bit as ugly as she could ever have thought. Their stone features were crushed and cracked, with great flattened noses and huge protruding eyebrows. It was clear that they had been designed to camouflage themselves on a mountainside, and successfully disguise themselves they had. Álfara thought desperately of anything she had ever read about Huldi. None of it was particularly helpful. It had mostly been about their appearance, and from the looks of things the descriptions had been far from accurate and had underrepresented them fiercely. During the great war between Kollungr and Einar, the Huldi had initially sided with the Dökkálfar until they saw Kollungr was going to lose, and then they had retreated to the mountains where no-one would bother them. It made sense that they found themselves at home in the Kaltspids which bordered the Norðurtre. They would have been stupid not to have had history with the Dökkálfar who had once lived right on their doorstep.

Describing the Huldi all it might, no book had ever told her how they might be defeated.

"What do we do?" Álfara whispered in her smallest voice to Pieni beside her. She glanced again at Nikkel who was still unconscious. "What will they do to us?"

"Depends on how they feel." Pieni muttered back, still speaking from the side of his mouth. "We were stupid not to have predicted they would have made their home here."

"This far down from the Kaltspids?" Álfara replied in spite of herself.

"Certainly. Do you think you and Nikkel are the only ones to sense the rising darkness?" Pieni opened his eyes and squinted up at Álfara from his balled-up position. He had a bloodied nose now that Álfara could see him properly, and it dripped into his snow-white beard. Somehow, the vulnerability of it all made him appear much less frightening and far older.

"What do the Huldi want?" Álfara asked. Her voice was a little louder than it had been before, and with a creak of rock against rock, the two Huldi looked their way. Pieni's eyes snapped shut in self-defence but it was too late for Álfara to do anything about it.

"Morning, starshine." The bigger, uglier Huldi said. He strode over to them and closed the gap in mere seconds. "Look who's awake."

"Got a splitting headache I don't doubt." Said his companion with a cruel laugh.

"No thanks to you." Álfara replied before she could stop herself. From all she had learned it seemed correct to answer with some form of braveness, although once the words had escaped her mouth it felt simply like stupidity.

The Huldi seemed to find it funny as they laughed their grating laughs and nudged each other with their rocky elbows.

"Ho-ho," said the larger, "Hark at the little Fe."

"How sweet!" replied his companion in a patronising tone.

"I'm not a Fe." Álfara replied indignantly, her jaw set.

"Not a Fe?" said the larger, "Then what are you, with your pointed ears and sparkling skin?!"

Out of the corner of her eye she saw Pieni twitch and knew he would be telling her to stop if he could speak, but she couldn't stop. At least if she kept the Huldi's attention it might give Pieni a chance to think of some form of escape for him, Töfrandi and Nikkel. She hoped Pieni knew that as she continued. Despite knowing the danger, she had to try.

"I'm a Ljósálfar, you ignorant paperweight." She forced herself to meet the bulging pebble eyes of the larger Huldi, staring him out.

The Huldi exchanged looks with each other, then looked back at her. If she didn't know better she would have said there was a touch of fear and admiration in their dead eyes.

"Are you really?" asked the second with an edge of curiosity to his gruff voice.

Álfara only managed to nod. Her fight seemed to be subsiding rapidly. The Huldi exchanged further glances.

"In that case," said the larger, "Höfðingi will want to speak with you."

Before Álfara could do anything else to stop them, the Huldi had each seized her firmly by the skinny elbows with their large hands and lifted her clean off her feet, carrying her from the frosted room with the ease of carrying a feather. She could not kick, she could not fight - all she could do was let them take her from her companions.

Pieni opened his eyes at the sound of Töfrandi's warning grunts. With a heavy heart, the Nisse realised that there was nothing anyone could do to help Álfara as she was dragged out of sight. All they could do was wait.

Álfara was roughly thrown down to the ground by her two captors. They were far taller than her and had been carrying her at some height, so it greatly hurt her to land on the ground with no means of protecting herself. She felt the shock in her ribs as her body collided with the stone and it took a moment for her to catch her breath. Above her head she could hear conversing in a language she did not understand. Huldin sounded just like the grating of stone on stone to her pointed ears. It was by no means a comfortable language to listen to, but despite not understanding a word she could sense the tone. The

Huldi who had captured them now seemed to be speaking with a third - Höfðingi perhaps - who spoke in a deeper voice than they. There was a sense of urgency to their conversation, and a great deal of questions judging from the back-and-forth and the tone.

"Very well," Höfðingi eventually said in the common tongue, "Leave her with me."

"Yes, chief." The two Huldi replied in unison. There was a crunching sound as they walked away, and Álfara tried once more to get to her knees. With no hands with which to balance it was not an easy task, but on her third try she managed to push herself up using her shoulders. It hurt greatly but at least now she was not as vulnerable and she could look upon this Höfðingi for the first time.

She was very surprised by what she saw as she raised her eyes to the direction his speech had originated.

Höfðingi was much taller than his Huldi companions, standing at almost 7 feet, but he was not as ugly. He had a big nose but he had grown a moss moustache beneath it, giving himself a far more refined look than the others. He wore a mantle of grasses upon his head and a long cloak of woven winter-flowers, which added some colour to his dark stone appearance. His dark pebbled eyes were almost curious as he surveyed the tiny Ljósálfar carefully.

"Is what they say true?" He asked in a low voice.

"Depends on what they say." Álfara replied. She stuck out her chin in defiance as that was the only gesture she could make. Höfðingi chuckled a little and stood up from his great stone chair. He took a step towards her, his heavy gait shaking the ground so that Álfara had to fight to stay standing. She held her resolve as best she could, however, when he peered down at her. Every swivel of his eyes was met with a grating rock-upon-rock sound that made her stomach squirm.

"A Ljósálfar." Höfðingi replied simply. He was looking especially at the ears exposed through her hair.

"Yes." Álfara responded. There was no use denying it when she did not have the means to cover her pointed ears.

"Why has a Ljósálfar come so far North?" Höfðingi asked with a stroke of his great mossy moustache.

Álfara swallowed hard. She did not know how to respond to his question. He, however, seemed to know the answer already.

"You are here for the lights, aren't you, and the one destined to banish the darkness? As it was told?" Höfðingi asked. Álfara's eyes widened in agreement before she could stop them, and Höfðingi smiled triumphantly.

"I knew it," was all he said.

11
Chapter Eleven
THE ONE WHO WAS PROMISED

11 | The One Who Was Promised

"I don't know what you mean." Álfara replied through a clenched jaw. She had never been good at lying, and it seemed that her attempt merely amused the Huldi chief. He smiled beneath his great moss moustache and folded his great stone arms.

"There has always been a legend of the one who was promised, the one who could banish the darkness once and for all. A descendant of Einar, it was said. Do you know of Einar?"

"Of course I do." Álfara replied, indignant in spite of herself.

"Good. Then you will know *he* was thought for a long time to be the one who was promised." With great effort, Höfðingi settled himself on the ground before Álfara. She was still bound by the ankles and wrists and was knelt awkwardly, although the chief lowering himself to her height gave her the chance to rest her neck somewhat. She frowned at him as he made himself comfortable.

"Was he not?" Álfara asked. She had heard the stories of the 'one who was promised'. Ljósálfar rarely spoke of the war, but when they did it was with great reverence about Einar. There had often been the question raised about why Einar was chosen to lead them into battle against Kollungr, to defeat the darkness, and it seemed to be the best explanation to say Einar had been chosen -

promised - by the Gods themselves. "He rid the world of the darkness as he was supposed to do." Álfara added, wanting to sound far less naive than she felt in the presence of Höfðingi, who was clearly a font of ancient knowledge.

Höfðingi chuckled again, the ground shaking.

"It is so like the Álfar to think themselves superior to all others." Höfðingi shook his head pityingly at Álfara in a way that made her prickle with anger. Who did he think he was to talk to her this way? Furthermore, how dare he simply call her *Álfar*. As far as the Ljósálfar were concerned this aligned their noble race with that of the Dökkálfar, and there was no deeper insult. To call them Álfar was to paint them both with the same brush and that was unforgivable. Höfðingi seemed to notice he had struck a nerve as he laughed a third time. Álfara glared at him in spite of herself and her vulnerability. She would not be insulted by a pile of rocks.

"Go on then." She replied curtly. "Tell me why Einar was not the promised one."

"The promised one was never going to be an Álfar - Ljósálfar or Dökkálfar." Höfðingi stroked his moustache as he surveyed her. He was speaking slowly to her as though she were stupid. "That could never be."

"And why not?" Álfara demanded. She would probably have folded her arms and stamped her foot had she been able.

"Because, little one…" Höfðingi gave her a patronising pat on her ringletted head. She tried to pull away but his great rock hand was too adept and she did not have the movement ability. "The Álfar races have always been unable to see what was right before their pointed ears. They have always been so selfishly caught up in their own superiority that every other race is beneath them."

"Do not confuse us with Dökkálfar, sir." Álfara's nostrils flared with anger. She could feel her cheeks flushing.

Höfðingi simply smiled at her in a patronising manner. "You are a contrite, blinded race. You think yourselves so high and mighty as you care for your animals and herd your shadows, but you are all so blind. Us Huldi, and the countless other races - Játte; Fe; Dverger - all those who have been swept up in the war between the Álfar for hundreds of years. We have never once failed to see what you cannot."

"Which is what?!" Álfara stared at Höfðingi with her hardest expression. She had learned it from her grandmother and felt a small pang of loss as she remembered this fact. She did not relent, however, her fists clenching where they rested. It was nothing short of a shock to learn that most of the races in Heimur felt this way about the Ljósálfar, the way they had always felt about the Dökkálfar. The part that hit her hardest was the reality of it all. With a twinge of guilt, Álfara realised that never once had she stopped to think about the other races. Höfðingi had a point in saying what he had about the Álfar being selfish... but then, if Einar wasn't the chosen one - who was? What had the Álfar failed to see? She had to know.

Höfðingi looked at Álfara for what felt like a long time. His dark eyes were filled with something resembling pity. She stared back at him, her breathing shallow. She had never once thought of herself as proud, but perhaps Höfðingi had another point there. Her fists clenched tighter so that her nails dug into her mittened palms. The Ljósálfar were an undeniably proud race - a trait she had despised in her own family and never once seen in herself - but was she, like they, also blinded by their selfishness? Were they no better than Kollungr and the Dökkálfar in thinking they were superior?

"If not an Álfar, then who is the one who was promised?" Álfara whispered in a tight voice. Anything to stop her evaluating her own worth.

Höfðingi simply raised his granite eyebrow in response. With a tight feeling engulfing her chest, Álfara realised she already knew the answer to her question without him having to speak it. It was plain as day and had been all along.

***

"*Nikkel!*"

The whisper was as loud as Pieni dared to make it. He tried to reach Nikkel with the tip of his boot, nudging as hard as he could with his squat foot outstretched. The Huldi who had dragged away Álfara had not returned, and so Pieni had taken the opportunity to upright himself from his ball position and try to gain a response from the Banvænn boy who was still unconscious beside him.

"Nikkel!" He hissed again, a little louder as his toes collided with Nikkel's own boot. With a resulting jerk and a gasp, Nikkel sat upright and blinked in the strange blue light of their frozen room. "Shh!" Pieni insisted as he watched Nikkel try to get his bearings.

The boy looked all around him, blinking a lot to clear his obviously foggy eyes, and then focused on Pieni. "Where's Álfara?" He demanded, his first thought of his dearest friend. He hadn't even taken time to take stock. It was only now, after his question was asked, that Nikkel realised his hands and ankles were bound. He gasped, and then gasped again when he saw Töfrandi miserably swinging upside-down high above them from the beam. "What's happening?"

"Huldi." Pieni said in a tight voice, spitting on the ground in front of him with disgust. There was a sizzle as his warm spit hit the icy ground.

"What are they?" Nikkel asked with a small frown on his rounding face, his expression one of command. This adventure seemed to have started ageing him rapidly. Where once he had resembled a cherub boy - rosy-cheeked and wide-eyed - he was now turning into a young man with furrows in his brow and the beginning of whiskers on his chin and upper lip. Pieni had only just realised this fact, and for a moment wondered if Álfara had noticed too. Nikkel was reaching the same comparable level of maturity as she was. It had only been about a month since Pieni had known them and even longer for Álfara and Nikkel since they had left Skógur Hanna Huldu, yet Nikkel already seemed to be becoming a young man. It was hard for Pieni to remember that Nikkel was so young and naive at times. He was still only 15 - an infant in any race besides Banvænn.

"Your people would call them 'trolls'," Pieni explained in a hushed sigh, "or Gonks, even. They're nasty creatures with rock hearts and rock souls. We use the term to insult stupid people in my own race."

"I've heard stories of them." Nikkel whispered, fear in his tone as he made the comparison. "They live in the mountains and resemble beings of stone. They're a legend... or they were."

"Well, they're real enough. Just like your friend Álfara. Legends are real, boy, and you need to come to terms with that." Pieni's voice was heavy with a tone of patronising warning.

"Where is she?" Nikkel demanded, his first question coming full circle.

"They took her." Pieni stated in gruff reality.

"Took her?" Nikkel bid. "Took her where?!"

"To Höfðingi, the chief, most likely." Pieni sniffed, his moustache quivering.

"Will she come to harm?" Nikkel was fighting against his restraints, filled with anguish at the thought of his friend alone with these terrifying Huldi. Any weakness within him, limited by his race, subsided in an instant.

"Shh!" Pieni urged as he tried to calm the boy. "She's smart. She'll be perfectly fine."

Nikkel looked at the Nisse, unsure if he himself believed the words he used to convince the Banvænn. Nonetheless he stopped struggling against the bonds around his wrists and ankles, and lowered his voice.

"What should we do?"

"Well," Pieni raised his eyes up to where Töfrandi hung melancholy above, "first things first - we need to get out of here."

Nikkel's brow furrowed at the sight of Töfrandi, once again noticing the poor beast strung up for the first time. Töfrandi grunted in reassurance as he slowly rotated around the beam. His antlers were no longer glowing fully. It seemed he did not have the strength. All he managed was the occasional burst of sparkling light that was not enough to do anything.

Nikkel frowned further as a sudden idea struck him.

"This is Hásætishöll, right?" He asked, casting his eyes around the dark stone room with its strange blue glowing light.

"Yes." Pieni agreed. "What's left of it."

"This *is* where the Guardians dwell?" Nikkel looked for any sign of them. There were none. Just black stone walls as far as Nikkel could see in the dim light.

"Yes." Pieni repeated, his voice slow and questioning as he tried to work out why Nikkel was asking.

"They told me to come here, Pieni." Nikkel said determinedly. "Somehow they want us here. Huldi or no Huldi."

"I don't think even the Guardians could predict the Huldi." Pieni shook his head so that his beard quivered. "They're tricksome beasts, Huldi. That's why they've lasted so long whilst so many haven't."

"Even so," Nikkel fought against his restraints with a renewed vigour and strength, "how could they not predict the Huldi? Do they not see all? Don't you see, this was meant to happen. They wanted us to come whether the Huldi were here or not." His eyes were wide and appealing as he looked at Pieni.

Pieni thought about it, his bushy white brow furrowing. There was a long silence as Nikkel watched the small, wrinkled face of his companion consider all options.

Finally, Pieni's watery eyes met Nikkel's expectant ones.

"What are you saying?"

Before Pieni could do anything more, however, Nikkel threw back his head and let out a shout at the top of his voice.

"What are you doing?!" Pieni hissed urgently, but it was too late. The damage was done. The sound of heavy rock footsteps from up above and all around resonated off the walls and ceiling as Huldi made their way in the direction of Nikkel's shout. "Are you crazy?!"

"Maybe." Nikkel said with a shrug, then threw back his head and shouted again, "Hej!".

The footsteps grew closer and Töfrandi lowed in an agitated fashion, surges of light radiating through his antlers.

Nikkel noticed it, and Pieni did too. It was more light than Töfrandi had managed in a long time. It was working, whatever this crazy plan of Nikkel's was. For a third time Nikkel shouted, "Hej!"

The footsteps were right outside the stone room within which they sat. Then, just as suddenly as Nikkel had shouted, the footsteps stopped and the lights in the room went out. The only sight was the casual glowing of Töfrandi's antlers from where he was up in the room. There was no sound except Nikkel's anticipatory breathing.

Then, in the silence, tiny lights burst into being. They were small at first, barely bigger than Pieni's fingernails.

As Nikkel watched they gradually grew stronger and larger, and seemed to be arranging themselves in a pathway.

"Liekki…" Pieni whispered in awe. Even the Nisse seemed stunned by the appearance of these lights, as if they were a myth even to him.

Nikkel didn't ask what that was. He didn't need to. The lights were making themselves known as they created pathways and danced around the companions. Almost immediately Nikkel felt his restraints break and, judging from the grunt to his side, Pieni's had too. The lights lifted to the ceiling and Töfrandi was soon released from his bonds and lowered the right way up onto the stone ground. Finally, the lights now glowing bright and dancing entrancingly, they formed a pathway to a stone doorway that now appeared in the rock walls.

Pieni looked at Nikkel as they stood, dusting themselves off.

"How did you know?"

"I'm here for a reason." Nikkel shrugged, absent-mindedly winding his fingers into the fur on Töfrandi's neck as though checking he was alright. "Huldi or no Huldi, the Guardians want me here..." Nikkel repeated.

With sure footing, he set out along the Liekki pathway towards the doorway. In that moment he was no longer the Banvænn boy who questioned the existence of Ljósálfar and Nissen. He had now become exactly who he had always meant to be.

The one who was promised.

12
Chapter Twelve
LIGHT IN THE DARKNESS

12 | Light in the Darkness

$\mathcal{T}$his was it. Everything that had happened over the last few months had led to this.

"Nikkel..." Álfara whispered with a look into Höfðingi's grey eyes, "He's the one who was promised?"

"Isn't it obvious?" Höfðingi asked with a rasping laugh. Álfara shifted against her restraints uncomfortably. How could she have been so blind? Of *course* Nikkel was the one who was promised. He was a Banvænn, it was true, but he was like no Banvænn Álfara had ever heard of. He had adventure in his spirit and

253

kindness in his soul. If anyone embodied the memory of Einar it was he. It was now abundantly clear to Álfara that her dreams had led to this moment, that everything she had ever thought aligned itself perfectly with Nikkel. She had dreamed of the Lights of the North so that she could be the one to accompany Nikkel here. She had experienced the darkness first hand so that she would have the drive to push him. She was not the promised one, but she was destined to guide the one who was.

"Why are you telling me this?" Álfara asked, her eyes narrowing as she looked at the great stone creature before her.

Höfðingi chuckled. Álfara was glad he found this all so amusing, someone should, but his constant ridicule was starting to really get on her nerves. She glared at him and waited for him to finish. As he stopped laughing, however, she saw a flicker of evil cross his face. He had been pleasant until now, but everything inside her told her this was ending.

"Because…" Höfðingi leaned close to Álfara so that his mouldy, moss-filled breath filled her senses, "the darkness is returning, and Kollungr promised us a place of our own if we helped stop the rising light."

Álfara felt a grip like an iron-vice around her heart. She had been a fool to trust a Huldi, she knew it, and yet she had considered doing it anyway. Höfðingi knew he had hit a nerve and, laughing infuriatingly once more, he picked Álfara up easily by her restraints and dragged her over to his throne.

"You came all this way for the Guardians of Knowledge, did you not?" Höfðingi asked as Álfara tried and failed to struggle from his grip. His rock form was too much for her slight frame. He threw her down before a pile of rubble that lay behind his stone chair. Álfara landed roughly on her front and felt the stones cut into her sparkling skin. She tossed back her hair and lifted her head to look at the rubble, her heart sinking as she saw a stone eye look back at her. "I killed the Guardians, girl. On Kollungr's orders there is nothing and no-one who can stop the darkness returning."

Álfara was silent. She took in the rubble before her and made out further features: claws; feathers; fur: all once made of the stone that now lay in powder. An Ulfur, a Björning and a Hvafn. Gone.

The Guardians of Knowledge were now nothing but dust.

Was there even any hope remaining?

***

The Leikki pathway led Nikkel, Töfrandi and Pieni out of their stone prison. The pathway was unfaltering, flickering slightly as the lights hovered and danced. There was no need for a lantern with their Leikki pathway, though Töfrandi's antlers glowed softly in the darkness of the stone corridor in which they now walked.

"I have heard of Leikki," Pieni whispered reverently, "but never thought I would see the day."

"Are they to be trusted?" Nikkel asked, faltering for the first time in his footing.

"Yes." Pieni replied. They passed a great pile of stone rubble that had once been a Huldi. "They seem to be on our side."

"The Leikki did that?!" Nikkel asked in-spite of himself. The Leikki lights danced in response. "You took down a whole Huldi?!" He was in awe. The Leikki lights danced again, agreeing. "Thank you." Another dance.

"Are you not afeared of them?" Pieni asked. His tone was the one now filled with awe.

"Should I be?" Nikkel asked in genuine question. "I am not Huldi?"

The Leikki danced around Nikkel's head as though speaking with him. Pieni glanced to Töfrandi, both of them unsure of what to make of the interaction or how to deal with Nikkel's new found superiority.

"No," Pieni agreed, "I suppose not."

Töfrandi grunted in concurrence.

They walked on in silence for a few moments, following the glimmering path of the Leikki. More stone piles lay either side of the path: Huldi defeated by the Leikki. They were illuminated by the Leikki, but there was another light shining upon them too. It took Pieni and Nikkel a moment to notice that Töfrandi's antlers grew brighter with every step he made. Pieni, upon realising, stopped still and stared at his Rensdyr friend.

"Töfrandi..." He whispered in a reverent tone. Töfrandi grunted again, a small smile in his bright eyes.

"What is it?" Nikkel asked, turning to face them. Pieni reached up and put a hand on Töfrandi's nose and Nikkel noticed tears in both of their eyes. "What?"

"Töfrandi has not glowed like this in so long." Pieni whispered. "We thought he would never glow like this again... not since..."

259

"Since what?" Nikkel asked.

Pieni looked at Nikkel. For the first time, he really looked at him.

Nikkel was nothing special. Not at first glance. He was a Banvænn boy of around 15. He was rounding in the face and shoulders and not overly tall. He wore threadbare clothing and a patchwork coat of emerald greens and maroon reds. He had tattered fur cuffs at his wrists and a collar at his neck. He had bright sparkling eyes and cheeks that grew rosy when he was agitated. He was sprouting whiskers on his lip and chin. He was nothing special, yet for the first time Pieni truly saw him.

"Since the light returned." Pieni replied. In one move, Pieni swept his long hat from his head and clutched it to his chest. Nikkel was taken aback by the gesture. "You are something truly marvellous, Nikkel." Pieni's beard swept the ground as he bowed before the boy. "You are the one who was promised, yes, but you are so much more."

"What do you mean?" Nikkel asked. There was an edge of fear to his voice now. He had never wanted or expected this. All he wanted, right now, was to find Álfara. He had paid no mind to his own destiny as he had blindly followed the Leikki path.

Pieni looked Nikkel in the eye.

"You are the light of the North... you have been all along. Forgive me for not seeing it sooner."

There was a moment of reverence as Nikkel drank in Pieni's words. Could he truly be that important? A boy from nowhere, of nothing.

"I just want to find Álfara and stop the darkness." Nikkel whispered. "That's all I want."

There was a sudden flurry of activity from the Leikki. They began to dance agitatedly, breaking the pathway and swirling around the companions as though telling them to be aware. Instinctively, Nikkel and Pieni both looked to the mounds of stone that had once been Huldi as though they were suddenly going to become Huldi once more. When they did not, they looked further afield. The Leikki seemed to be surging forwards in waves, urging them to hurry down the pathway that they had created.

"Come on." Nikkel whispered in a gruff voice. He was touched by Pieni's loyalty, it was true, but they had a job to do. They had to find Álfara before it was too late, but first...

Something in the stone wall caught Nikkel's eye as they hurried along. He stopped and reached out for it. He didn't know how, or why, but he knew he needed it.

***

"What kind of fool built their Heimur bound vessels from simple stone?" Höfðingi threw back his head and laughed the hardest at his own joke as Álfara . "Stone can easily be destroyed, as was proved when my Huldi and I smashed the Guardians of so-called Knowledge to pieces. Did they fight back?" He threw back his head and barked a laugh again, "Did they Hel!"

"Why would you do that?" Álfara asked. She struggled up to her knees, using her shoulders as leverage to push herself to some form of upright. Her wrists were beginning to chafe where the ropes rubbed against them.

Her skin was delicate at the best of times and the Huldi ropes were rough and knotted.

"Why?!" Höfðingi rolled his eyes with a disgusting, stomach-turning stone-on-stone sound. "Because! We had to get to the light and defeat it."

"The light isn't a physical thing." Álfara argued in spite of herself. She couldn't seem to help it: Höfðingi was right, she was a proud Ljósálfar.

"Do you not know anything?" Höfðingi scratched his head as though genuinely confused by the Ljósálfar's ignorance. Álfara blinked at him, faltering in her assurance. Höfðingi was right, infuriatingly. She didn't know anything. Not really. But she wouldn't let that defeat her. Höfðingi seemed to be amused by her expression. "The light of the Guardians, their spirit as it were, was contained in a vessel. That vessel was kept in the centre of these stone statues. Only, they abandoned their posts. They no longer possessed the statues when we got here. Couldn't be bothered, probably. The vessel was there for the taking."

"What was the vessel?" Álfara asked with a frown. She looked around for fragments of smashed glass or crystal, anything except stone. She could hardly look at the remnants of the Guardians. She couldn't believe it. Wouldn't. Surely such ancient beings wouldn't just leave such an important vessel unattended.

"A Stjarna. One of the last remaining on Heimur, I'd wager." Höfðingi unceremoniously pulled up his great mossy trousers as though the conversation was boring him. He yawned to hammer home his point. Yet, there was a confusion in his tone now not gone unnoticed by Álfara.

"So you smashed it?" She asked, choosing her words carefully.

"We did... or at least, we nearly did." Höfðingi said through his yawn. He then seemed to realise what he said and glared at her. "Enough questions. Your Guardians are gone, Álfar. Your hope is lost. The light cannot return without the vessels and the Guardians who protected it."

"Only they didn't." Álfara said. Höfðingi nodded, though he seemed to have neglected to notice Álfara's tone. Her mind was racing. The Guardians couldn't have abandoned their post: she knew it. They didn't, she was sure of it. These stone statues had been just that: stone. The Stjarna that contained the light had not been smashed by the Huldi because they had not been able to find it. That was what Höfðingi was telling her, and that was all she needed to know.

"Enough questions." Höfðingi repeated in a grunt. He picked Álfara up by her chafing wrists again and began to drag her towards the door. She didn't fight him. She, instead, used what was left of her energy on formulating a plan. The Stjarne containing the light was here somewhere, in Hásætishöll. It had to be. Why else would the Huldi still be here? Kollungr, if he was indeed returning, had promised the Huldi darkness and a place to dwell, but he would not pay up upon his return unless he could be sure that they had done their part. That was why there were great stone tunnels beneath the fortress: they were looking for the Stjarne that held the light. What was more, Höfðingi had all but confirmed that Kollungr was returning in some form or another. Could that happen? Could he rise from the dead after all this time? Were they all truly in danger?

Álfara suddenly saw something out of the corner of her eye that gave her hope. She smiled as it reflected in her emerald eyes. It did not seem as though Höfðingi had noticed.

"You said it yourself, Höfðingi," She said in a quiet voice. Höfðingi grunted in response as he continued to drag her across the rocky ground, "Stone can easily be destroyed."

"What are you getting at...?" Höfðingi stopped walking and looked down at her. She was smiling in a way that unsettled him. He had no more chance to speak, however, as the Leikki swarmed him. Álfara launched herself from the flurry using her legs. She rolled roughly along the ground, grunting as she did, and came to a stop just in time to see the stones that were once Höfðingi crumble to the pile of rubble they deserved to be.

"Why make vessels of stone?" She said quietly to herself as one of his stone eyeballs rolled past where she lay.

"Álfara!"

Nikkel was upon her almost immediately, untying her sore wrists and pulling her gently to her feet.

"Nikkel!" Álfara cried, throwing her arms around his neck.

"I thought I'd never see you again!" Nikkel said into the curls that lay on Álfara's neck.

"And I you," Álfara whispered, holding him tightly. She then held him at arms length and looked into his eyes. "Nikkel, I have so much to tell you!"

"Me first!" Nikkel replied, straightening Álfara's hat as he held her before him. "My dreams, they came true. We were right, the darkness is coming.

"Kollungr, he's coming back." Álfara nodded.

"We have to stop him!" Nikkel gasped.

"You do," Álfara corrected him, "You're the one that was promised..." Álfara agreed, relaying what she had learned from the pile of rubble that used to be the Huldi chief. "You have to stop the rising darkness, Nikkel."

Nikkel faltered.

"I don't think I can do it alone." He whispered, his courage subsiding as he looked at his dearest friend.

"You won't have to." Pieni spoke from behind them. Álfara looked over to him and Töfrandi, hurrying to hug them. She stopped when she saw Töfrandi's antlers.

"Töfrandi!" She gasped, throwing her arms around him. He breathed in agreement, his breath warm on her pointed ears. "You're glowing!"

"It's Nikkel. He has brought back Töfrandi's power." Pieni said, nodding proudly. "Nikkel *is* the Light of the North."

"What?" Álfara frowned at Pieni, then turned to Nikkel. "How? Höfðingi said it was a Stjarne...?"

In answer, Nikkel opened his fist. Held in it, glowing slightly in the light from the Leikki, was a small silver crystal.

"The Stjarne is just a vessel." Pieni explained, as he had done to Nikkel when he had plucked the silver glowing thing from the wall. "It contains the Light, but that is all. Somehow, someway, sometime it transferred to Nikkel."

"That's why I've been having dreams, Álfara." Nikkel said. "Pieni told me. Once we found the Stjarne, it was obvious. When the Huldi came here to fight the Guardians of Knowledge and take the Stjarne containing the light, the light had fled. It had sought a new vessel."

"Not just any. The promised vessel." Pieni corrected.

Nikkel shifted uncomfortably, clearly not comfortable with this description.

"Then…" Álfara frowned. "Why has it been asking you to come to Hásætishöll? Why make you travel all this way if it was with you already?"

Suddenly, all the light in the room went out.

13
Chapter Thirteen
THE PROTECTOR

13 | The Protector

$\mathcal{A}$ sudden wind began to build in the darkness. Even Töfrandi's antlers had stopped glowing, and the Leikki had fled. Fragments of ice and snow began to blow around them, caught by the wind and thrown at them like glass. Álfara flinched as one cut her cheek and raised her hand to shield her eyes from the onslaught.

"Nikkel?!" Álfara cried out fearfully.

"I'm here."

Álfara felt his fingers close around hers in reassurance. She could hear his teeth chattering against the sudden wind.

"Pieni?" Álfara called.

No response.

"Pieni!?" Nikkel called a little louder.

Silence.

Then out of the darkness came a cry that chilled Nikkel and Álfara to the bone. It was a scream that shook the air around them.

"Pieni!" They shouted together.

"Get out of here!" Pieni shouted from somewhere in the pitch black. "Get the Light of the North to safety."

"What does he mean?" Nikkel asked, his voice shaking.

"You!" Álfara pushed Nikkel in the direction of what she hoped was the way they had come in. "He means you! We have to get you out of here!" They broke into a run, their hands still clutched, but stopped when Nikkel screamed.

"What is it?!" Álfara turned to face him in the darkness. She could see his face now, lit by the glowing of the Stjarne he had held in his hand moments before. It was now dropped and skittering across the stone.

"It burned me!" Nikkel explained, shouting over the rising wind and storm swirling about them.

"Pieni! I thought you said it was just a vessel! It contains it but that's all!" Álfara cried desperately, not sure if Pieni would even hear her.

"Somehow it still contains the light! I was wrong!" Pieni shouted back. "Get out of here!"

"What about the Stjarne! We need it!"

Álfara felt Nikkel release her hand as he dived into the snowstorm to retrieve the glowing Stjarne.

"Nikkel!" Álfara shouted. "Come on!"

She suddenly felt something slam into her back from behind, sending her flying to the ground. A second blow was heard, and Nikkel plummeted to the stone floor just before her. She could see his outline in the glowing light of the Stjarne.

"What was that?!" Álfara cried.

"Myrkur!" Pieni cried from somewhere in the darkness. They heard Töfrandi bray in response and the sound of their companions fighting something unseen. "Grab the Stjarne and get out of here!"

"Not without you!" Nikkel shouted back.

"Don't argue with me!" Pieni shouted through gritted teeth. "Someone needs to stop Kollungr! The Lights of the North are the only way to do that. I failed before, I will not fail now: my destiny is with you two! Now stop arguing! Take it and run!"

Nikkel and Álfara looked at each other in the glow of the Stjarne light, the only in the room. Their vision of each other was obscured by the swirling snowflakes and ice cutting their faces. Nikkel's cheeks were bright red in the cold and the tips of Álfara's ears crimson. Neither could stand with the force of the wind buffering them and pinning them to the ground. Álfara dug her curled boots into the stone floor and managed a small shuffle forward, closer to the glowing Stjarne. Nikkel saw her reach out.

"Take it Álfara!" Nikkel shouted over the sound of the whooshing, whirring, pulsating. "Take it and run!"

"No!" Álfara shouted back, her face a mask of fear and her fist clenching around the air. "I won't leave you!"

"There is no sense in both of us failing!" Nikkel's voice was filled with desperation, his eyes pleading. "Please! You're closer, you take it and run! I'll be right behind you!"

Álfara's green eyes filled with tears as she looked through the swirling snows to her friend. His own grey eyes were wide and hopeful as he looked back at her, his entire expression telling her that it was okay - this was what was meant to happen. Perhaps they had all been wrong. He wasn't the promised one, she was, and they had ignored it so fervently. There was no denying it now. She had been the one to read the book on Einar's descendants. She was the stronger race, the Ljósálfar. Light was in her destiny.

"I don't want to leave you." Álfara sobbed, her voice a barely audible whisper in the roaring maelstrom.

Nikkel offered her a small smile, one that clearly took all of his courage to produce. There was little more that he could do.

"I will find you. We will make it out of this, defeat the darkness." He promised, his eyes shining as he, too, fought back tears. "I made you a promise, didn't I? Believe in me?"

Álfara gazed for a moment into his earnest face. Slowly, taking all of the strength she possessed, Álfara nodded. She was smaller and could run easier in this wind. She had to be the one to take it to safety, to run. To never stop running, no matter how long it took.

"I will always believe in you." She whispered through a forced smile. Then, in one definitive moment, and with her eyes fixed upon those of her closest companion, Álfara's long elven fingers closed around the Stjarne.

All went black.

There was no sound, no wind, nothing.

The only thing Álfara could be sure of in her new pitch-like suspension was the sound of her heart, beating as it was in her pointed ears. For a moment she let herself float where she was, suspended in this nothingness. This darkness.

Then, as soon as she forced her eyes open, the floating sensation ceased and she plummeted several feet down flat onto her back. Álfara let out an involuntary moan as all of the air was thrust from her lungs. It took her a further moment to take stock. She was alive, or at least... she was aware. She was no longer in that room with the swirling snows and rough winds. The darkness was just as ruthless outside of her eyelids. She scanned the pitch black with her glittering orbs. Nothing. She was lying flat on her back in the middle of nothing and nowhere. Her heart was beating, so she must still be alive, but what was this existence? Was it even existing at all?

Álfara forced herself to sit up, or at least try to, though it was hard to know which way was up or down when all was emptiness.

Not all. She was flesh, and in her hand... it was still squeezed tightly shut. Yet, as she tried to focus her vision upon her own fingers, she could make out a faint blue glow from the space between each one. She held the Stjarne to her chest protectively, though what was there to protect it from?

Hardly daring to believe this light in the darkness, her heart pounding louder and her hand trembling, Álfara opened her fingers.

The Stjarne was still clutched in her hand. Surely that meant something. She had intended to grab it and escape, that was what she had been told, but not like this. She had been transformed, transported, and here she was far away from, well, anywhere. What was this darkness? Where was she? Had she escaped?

Álfara closed her fingers around the Stjarne once again and, her legs trembling, climbed shakily to her feet. Her head was clearing a little now, although it was still difficult to take stock of anything when all was nothing.

Where was Nikkel?

Where were Pieni and Töfrandi?

Where was the Hásætishöll with its room of rubble?

Where was *she*?

Suddenly, in answer to Álfara's unspoken questions, there came a sound from over to her right. It was far away in the darkness, but it was unmistakable. It was the sound of armour, and it was getting closer.

Every sense in her body told her that she had to go, to run. But where? She didn't even know where she was, let alone where she could go.

Clutching the light to her chest protectively, Álfara turned to her left and started to run. Yet it was as though she were running in a dream. She moved her feet and her legs but she did not move any further forwards.

Laughter.

There was laughter behind her, in time with the clanking armour.

This was exactly like her dream.

Was she dead?

No.

A dark voice inside her head. It was not her own. She had never heard it in waking memory.

You are not dead. But you are trapped here.

Who are you?! Álfara shouted inside her own mind.

Nothing but laughter responded. It resounded in her mind until she had to stop running and curl up into a ball. It was too loud. It possessed her every thought.

Forwards. Walk forwards, now.

Álfara's eyes snapped open at this new, softer, voice. She did as she was told without question, taking one step and then another. She found this time she could quite easily walk forwards. She tried to keep herself calm as she walked, hearing the endless laughter and clank of armour vanish behind her.

See the light?

She could. There was daylight up ahead. It took everything inside her not to run towards it. The light didn't move away.

Still with the Stjarne clutched to her chest, Álfara's shaking legs carried her towards the light.

It was a doorway, an opening in this dark cave. She stepped through it, blinking in the light. Daylight. Sunlight.

A moment, and then Álfara stopped walking and looked around her. The ground was spongy grass beneath her feet. The slight breeze of forest air brushed her bruised cheeks and ruffled her curls. Her clothes were torn from the storm and she clutched her coat around her as she took stock. She was outside of a great stone cave on a rolling green hill. There, just ahead of her, were great green tents bearing the emblem of a sun and star.

Soldiers in armour of the brightest gold walked to and fro, the emblem emblazoned proudly upon their metal suits. A commander stood just before Álfara with his head surveying a great map of Heimur. He had flowing golden hair and his skin shone brighter than any Álfara had ever seen amongst her own kind. A small crown of woven gold was set upon his head.

Einar.

Álfara pinched herself. She was no longer dreaming. This was real.

Whatever had happened in that cave had sent her back in time. Hundreds of years, in fact. Back in time to defeat the darkness, and here she was at the summit of Einar's war camp just metres from Einar himself.

With a pang in her heart she thought of Nikkel, Pieni and Töfrandi back in the future where she had been forced to leave them. She had not wanted to and rightly it made no sense. Nikkel was the chosen one, not she, yet here she was. She, Álfara, had been sent back in time for a reason. The protector.

To defeat Kollungr and banish the darkness once and for all.

The first step was always going to be the hardest. She could do it, she knew she could. She may not be the promised one but Álfara was the last of the Ljósálfar.

Álfara just had to take the first step.

The End.

The Chronicles of Álfara

will continue in

Book Two: *The Sands of Time.*

Printed in Great Britain
by Amazon

18519121R00169